A Notable Woman

DON ANDERSON

The views expressed in this book are solely those of the author and do not necessarily reflect the views of the publisher, and the publisher hereby disclaims any responsibility of them.

Olympus Story House

Table of Contents
DEDICATION

DEDICATION

To three very special/notable women.

First, to my wife of fifty-three years (that fact alone makes her a very special/notable woman), for her honest appraisal and feedback without which this book may have never been completed.

Second, to my friend, Lydia Donohue, a fellow Christian and editor, who spent countless hours editing this book, making suggestions in grammar and helpful recommendations on ow that were what I felt were Holy Spirit inspired. Thank you.

Third, to Jelene Speder, who is also my friend and fellow Christian who also helped edit and graciously gave me great insights for the book. Thank you.

INTRODUCTION

Several years ago, a minister friend asked me a question that I had not been asked before: "Do you have a hero? Someone that inspires you more than anyone else?"

I answered, "I hadn't thought about it, but I will give your question some serious thought."

As I begin to consider his question, my thoughts naturally opened to inspiring individuals of the Bible—people like Abraham who journeyed to an unknown land after he heard a command from God whom he did not know. Or teenage David who fought and killed a giant of a man for insulting God and, against all odds, became King of Israel. Or even Esther who became queen of the mightiest nation on earth at that time and then risked her life to save her people. There were so many others I could have picked as a personal hero, but the worthy choice for my hero was actually a heroine, an unnamed woman… not a war hero. She didn't save a nation, she didn't give birth to any other major biblical character, and she wasn't even Jewish; yet her profound story took up the major portion of two chapters in the Bible. You will find her fascinating story beginning in 2 Kings 4:8 and continuing in 8:1. The Bible simply refers to her as the Shunammite woman. But here, for the purpose of telling her story and to help make it come alive, I will call her Marta, which means in ancient Aramaic "lady of the house."

Over the years, I have not heard a message about her except one I spoke, and it was the first sermon I ever preached as an ordained minister. Since that time, over twenty years ago, I have committed myself to bring the Shunammite woman to literary life. My aim is to unveil her heart the same way God revealed her to me in my mind's eye. To tell her story as He showed me by reading between the lines.

As you read this story, remember she is a Gentile, not Jewish, so her reaction to various situations will customarily be different from Jewish heroes you read about in the Old Testament.

Writing her story has been a heartwarming adventure. The Holy Spirit has been unrelenting, gently prodding until one day, after some years, I sensed His tap on my shoulder and His whisper in my ear, "It's time, you must tell her story!" So finally, here it is… *A Notable Woman.*

PART 1
2 Kings 4:8–37

1
Coming of Age

It was early spring in the year 835 BC in a region near the coast of Israel called the plain of Sharon. In the middle of that plain was an ancient royal Canaanite city called Shunem located at the base of a large hill. The town had a mystical air about it; dirt roads lined with date palm trees carried wagons and carts into the city loaded with goods of all kinds, including huge stacks of hay and baskets of vegetables. They were drawn by mules, some by horses or oxen, but most were drawn by small donkeys pulling loads that looked far too large for them. Camels carried oversized loads of rugs, wooden boxes, large cakes of salt, and more. Women could be seen carrying baskets and large clay vessels on their heads while men herded sheep, camels, and cattle form one area of the valley to another. This peaceful and prosperous city relied mainly on agriculture for their main industry.

It was midafternoon on a beautiful day; the sun was shining, and there wasn't a cloud in the sky. The hills around the city were covered with grass and trees reflecting the fertile soil and generous rainfall in the region. Sheep and cattle in abundance grazed in open pastures, and there were freshly plowed fields that surrounded the city. Plowmen could be seen and heard cursing their oxen that were laboring under their burdens.

A large wall, thirty feet tall and five feet thick, surrounded the city on all four sides. Four large oak-beam gates were at the entrances of each side: north, south, east, and west. Along the wall were several towers guarding the city from any dangerous enemies. Two main roads trodden with animal traffic wandered through Shunem from gate to gate. Brown dust was stirred and ascended from the roads as the carts and wagons ambled to various places of business.

Just inside the western wall of the city was a house surrounded by a dozen trees inside a ten-foot wall. Sitting on the back steps of the house in the shade of a fig tree was a young girl, a very special girl. A girl named Marta meaning "lady of the house."

Marta was tall and thin; had thick, long jet-black hair and hauntingly beautiful large gray eyes. She was not lanky as are most teenagers but walked with a grace that was far beyond her years. She always stood tall with self confidence and poise that made her stand out in a crowd. When she entered a room, everyone noticed, and conversations would stop as all attention would focus on her. Marta was intelligent, had a quick mind, and could size up situations in very short order. She could outthink all her friends to the point that none would openly challenge her in an argument. Any adult who would challenge her thoughts and opinions soon found themselves throwing up their hands, laughing and walking away, shaking their heads. She was strong-willed but respectful and polite, a born leader—not that she went out of way to be— she just was.

On this warm spring day, while sitting on the back steps, Marta was contemplating the implications of having just turned sixteen and was feeling on top of the world. At that time, in her culture, a girl of sixteen years old was considered to be adult and could attend parties and special functions with the other adult women and be involved in their discussions and other adult privileges. She resented the countless times she would be unceremoniously sent outside so the women could have an "adult conversation." In her frustration, she would kick the ground and mutter to herself and obediently leave. It was so exciting now to be in that special women's club and be a part of those secret conversations that were reserved for adults only. She couldn't help but slip into adolescent daydreams about all the implications of her new status. The typical young teenage issue seized her being as a young woman living between two worlds; in one world, she was an adult and in the other, an exuberant teenager. In one world, she was a child who still liked toys, and in the other, she was a grown-up woman expected to lay the toys aside.

Marta lived in a large gray and tan house built with stone, timbers, and mud bricks with fronds covered with mud for a roof. The roof was flat and a welcoming place where the family would spend summer evenings in the cool of the day to enjoy the breezes and beautiful sunsets. The house had large beam-framed windows, and the doors were made of thick oak boards and had heavy iron hinges. The front and back porches were narrow and made of wood and each had three steps leading up to their respective doors.

Even though they lived within the walls of the city, her father felt a little more exposed than he liked and was worried about nefarious characters that lurked just outside the city walls. He felt his house was more exposed to the dangers of these bad characters than houses in the center of the city, so he build a ten-foot-high mud and stone wall around their house and garden. Marta's mother was named Sonta, her father named Akeem, and two younger brothers, twelve and ten years old, all shared this home along with ve servants.

Daydreaming, Marta was feeling a bit self-important as she was making all sorts of life plans in her mind. Just at that time, she heard her mother call out, "Marta, where are you?" The voice woke her out of her imaginings.

"I am on the back steps, Mama." The sound in her mother's voice bothered her. "You sound angry. Is everything all right? Am I in trouble?"

Her mother responded, "Yes, yes, everything is all right, and no, you are not in trouble. I just need you in here."

Her mother sounded both irritated and stressed. "Come in now and help me with supper. You need to remember that you are not a child anymore. You have responsibilities. Now get to them. I shouldn't have to remind you all the time. Now, I need you to take over grinding the wheat for bread."

The other side of what it meant to be considered an adult was also just beginning to dawn on Marta. Along with the tantalizing privileges came the mundane life of chores and responsibilities. Life wasn't going to be all about sweet-smelling owers and feelings of self-importance but included the more tedious day-to-day duties and expectations as well.

Marta took a deep sigh and called out, "Coming, Mama."

She stood up, brushed her dress off, and ran into the house and into the kitchen. It was a large room with three tables for preparing food and for the servants to eat at. In a corner, there was a round oven for baking bread, and in the center of the room, there was a type of stove made of a circle of at rocks and across the top was a grate of brass and a at brass pan.

Her mother looked over at her and said, "Hurry up, we are having a visitor coming for dinner. Where is your shawl? You are a young woman now. It is not proper to go around with your head uncovered."

Sonta was always stressed when her husband's visitors came. She knew that the way she performed her duties directly reflected on her husband, his business, and the family's status in the community. Marta took her shawl from around her shoulders and pulled it over her head. As she walked into the room, she could smell the sweet aroma of hot bread, roasted meat, and spices permeating the air. Her mother was an excellent cook.

Sonta was tall, somewhat thick around her middle, and had long thin arms and legs. Her skin was light brown, and her face was pretty but with a time worn hardness about it. Her hair had tinges of gray at the temples and was pulled back under a red and gray linen shawl. She was a kind woman, but firm. Her children adored her.

She was hard at work, grinding wheat to make more bread when Marta came in the kitchen. Marta immediately took over the grinding so her mother could go on to other things. The sound of grinding grain with a stone mortar and pestle was pleasing to the girl.

"Is everything all right?" Marta asked again. "You seem to be stressed. Is it because of who is coming to visit?"

"Saana is coming, and whether I am stressed or not is no concern of yours. Just grind the grain for now. There's still a lot to do, and I fear he will be here before I can get everything ready," she lamented.

"Yes, Mama, I will work as fast as I can."

A chill went up Marta's back and a knot developed in the pit of her stomach when her mother mentioned Saana's name. She did not like him. He was mean to his servants and was rude, crass, and ugly—so ugly. Saana was nearing fifty but looked much older. He was an extremely successful farmer whom her father admired.

Anyone with money was highly respected by Akeem; Saana had an abundance of money and was considered the richest person in the region.

Saana was a thin, shorter man, a bit shorter than Marta. His long, chest length, salt-and-pepper beard didn't hide his leathery, pock-scared face and sunken cheeks. He was missing three front teeth and the ones he had were brownish gray. His voice was high-pitched and an awful shrill pierced the atmosphere when he shrieked through his thin lips. His breath was foul, and one could smell it from a distance. He was truly an unpleasant man.

Up until recently, Saana rarely visited Marta's house and never for supper, but about two years ago, his visits started to be much more frequent, and with each visit, he stayed longer and usually for the evening meal. He often came unannounced, and her father disliked his rude, unannounced visits but unexplainably tolerated them. Saana was offensive, and Akeem awkwardly fawned over him while he was in the house—to a point that it made her father look ridiculous. Se one issue about Saana that bothered Marta more than all others, even more than his coarseness, was his constant gawking at her. Occasionally, he would smile at her, with his ragged toothed smile and cold eyes, and it would make her shiver with fear and revulsion. She would avert her eyes and not look directly at him again for the rest of the evening.

Marta's father, Akeem, was a tall man, with a medium, somewhat muscular build, and had a jet-black beard with ecks of gray. He had a thin, hard face, a heavy brow, and dark brown eyes. Though he was a good provider, he was not an affectionate father. He almost completely ignored Marta and the rest of the children, saying, "I'm a busy man. Children are for the woman to care for. I don't have the patience."

As a merchant, Akeem bought and sold linen and raw cotton. He would regularly go as far as Egypt on buying trips, traveling to Egypt as many as two or three times a year and then to Jerusalem, Nazareth as well as other towns and cities in the region buying and selling his products. Being a somewhat shrewd man, he often appeared gruff but watched over his children more than they realized. He was aware and even proud of their talents and abilities but said very little about them to anyone.

Akeem was a hardworking man and had little patience with lazy people. Financially, the family was better off than most in her community, but by no means were they numbered among the rich.

Saana, on the other hand, was rich, very rich. Outside the city, he owned several large fields where there stood five impressive barns made with stone walls and timber roofs. Close to the barns, he had a large, two-story flat-roofed house built with stone and timbers, and the house was covered in a plaster/mud mix. Several beautiful large trees surrounded the house. The farm was maintained by more than two dozen overworked servants most of which worked the fields.

Even though he owned a massive amount of sheep, cattle, and other farm animals, the one thing he didn't have was a wife and children. A family—heirs to pass on his legacy. When asked about his marital status, he would sarcastically reply, "I'm too busy for a wife right now. I don't need a silly woman to take up my time and especially my money, and I hate children."

Two years earlier, one of Saana's business associates brought up the subject of marriage again and asked him, "Who is going to inherit all this wealth you've accumulated? Your sons? You have none. You need to get married and have sons. All these riches and the land you have amassed will be stolen by your enemies if you don't have a son. They will lie and say you owed them money; they will form plots and vouch for each other. The king, who by the way is no friend of yours, will give them your land because there is no one else to claim it. You have no heir to fight for it.

The idea sobered Saana. In his self-centeredness, he neglected to make any plans past his own mortality. His conscience began to work on his shortsighted, selfish nature, and he realized that he couldn't take it with him, and he needed a beneficiary. He could not stomach the idea of anyone else, especially any of his enemies— of which he had many—getting their hands on his possessions. He wasn't reasoning about the benefit to a son as much as his own selfish pride and keeping it away from his enemies. Saana didn't have an altruistic bone in his body.

That day, he made up his mind that he would take a wife, but who? He had a problem, a serious problem. Though he was rich, his well-deserved reputation as a hard, dishonest, and cruel man was not trusted by those in the city, and especially not trusted by anyone who knew him personally. Over the years, he had, at one time or another, by a little or by a lot, cheated nearly every businessman in town. Even his wealth could not sway parents to give him one of their daughters for marriage. His evil reputation prevented parents from accepting even large sums of money for their daughter, fearing that he would somehow cheat them or renege on his agreement because of all the strings he would invariably attach.

However, there was that one daughter, the daughter of a certain linen merchant whose name was Marta who was strikingly beautiful. Unfortunately, she was currently too young for marriage. Sixteen was the customary marrying age for girls, and Marta was only fourteen years old. When no one would make marriage arrangements with him, he had no other alternative but to try and bargain with Akeem for his daughter's hand. Saana decided he would approach the girl's father and arrange a marriage, offering an exceptionally large sum of money, and with most of that up front and in gold. Saana played on the fact that he had learned the father was having severe financial problems caused by a drought in Egypt. Akeem's ominous circumstance presented a perfect opportunity for Saana to haggle with him. After days of negotiations and with lots of money offered (with no strings), Akeem agreed that Saana and Marta would marry in two years when she became of age. Saana had waited a long time, so a little longer would not unsettle him at all. After all, he was not planning on dying anytime soon.

His self-serving logic, largely birthed out of a sense of desperation, convinced Saana that this was his best and truly his only option. When he, at first, presented the proposal, Akeem was hesitant; but when Saana offered him a fortune in gold up front, as proof of his earnest intentions, Akeem was shaken. Seeing the gold in front of him and considering his grievous nancial situation, Akeem finally gave in and agreed to the "arrangement." Although full of misgivings, he knew he really had no other choice. A local elder was brought in as a witness, and the deal was agreed on and an approximate date set—a date sometime shortly after Marta's sixteenth birthday.

*****

The two years had passed quickly, and the time for the marriage had come. Both Marta and her mother were completely in the dark about Akeem's business "arrangement" with Saana—that was until this day.

Saana showed up for supper with two servants and a growling disposition. "It's late. Do you have supper ready? I hope it's something I can eat this time. The last time I was here, the meal was just tolerable." Sonta tried not to react to his insults, his rudeness, and terrible demeanor. She hoped to calm him with a quiet voice, a forced smile, and by offering him wine, which he took with a grunt. Marta caught a disgusted look in her mother's eye. It was the first time she realized her mother detested this terrible man maybe even more than she did. Sonta was mystified as to how her husband could allow this rude and uncouth man in their house, let alone tolerate Saana's horrible behavior without saying something. She felt that Saana was one of the most despicable humans she had ever seen or even heard of.

Akeem was fawning over Saana like he was a king. Her father started shouting orders to his wife and daughter like they were the lowest of servants. Marta absolutely hated being treated like a slave. She loved to serve people and felt waiting on friends was one of the best ways to show her appreciation for their friendship, but to be treated like a slave, the lowest of servants, she deeply detested. She never treated any of the servants that way and only tolerated Saana's poor treatment for her mother's sake. Marta knew that if she said anything, not only would she suffer a beating but her mother as well, who would try and defend her.

Saana's servants, with their eyes downcast, neither moved from his side nor spoke a word. The empty look in their eyes revealed they were broken and without hope; they had surrendered themselves to a life of misery.

The girl felt pity for them. She thought to herself, *I wish I could help them. They look so sad. How my heart aches for them. I wish there were something I could do to help them.* Little did she know that the opportunity to do just that was only a few months away.

Saana and Akeem sat down to supper and were waited on hand and foot by Sonta, Marta, and their servants. The whole time they were eating, the men held conversations like there was no one else in the room. Marta and her mother were completely ignored. It was as though they didn't exist except to serve. Saana cleared his throat loudly and, with his broken-toothed smile, brought up "the arrangement."

"Well, when do we finalize the arrangement?" Saana asked with an officious tone.

"Now is as good a time as any," Akeem replied.

Marta's mother had a surprised look; she looked at her husband quizzically and then a look of realization came on her face. She glanced over to the girl with a terrified look that caused chills to run down Marta's spine. Marta knew something bad was about to happen, but she couldn't figure out what it could possibly be. Was her father going into partnership with this terrible man? What could disturb her mother so much?

"Good," said Saana, and he looked at the girl with a smile that made her curious and repulsed at the same time. Slowly, she was beginning to realize what was about to happen. It couldn't be! Her father and her were never close, but this was unfathomable. She felt like her father was about to pronounce a death sentence over her. Akeem's next words felt as if a mountain had fallen on her.

Marta's father cleared his throat and said, "We can make the marriage arrangements for four months from today." Then he went on to say, "It will take that long to arrange the wedding ceremony and the feast."

Marta's mother fell to her knees and was pale as a ghost. The young girl's heart was beating so hard she thought it was going to burst. The room started to spin around her, and sweat developed on her forehead. The next thing Marta knew she was looking up from the floor. One of Saana's servants was holding her head and the other servant her hand. The look on their faces was one of extreme pity. The servant holding her head saw Marta's look of sympathy for them when they walked in; now he reasoned her situation was far more terrible than his.

He said in a quiet voice, "We will look out for you—we will help you."

It was a nightmare—worse than a nightmare, it was real. No words could comfort her. She tried to fathom what was happening, but she couldn't get past those appalling words: "marriage arrangements." All the daydreams she had about being an adult, accompanying her mother to those special "secret women's meetings," all the joys of womanhood vanished with this disgusting reality. Not only did fear and despair permeate her being, but deep feelings of hopelessness seemed to also choke out every good thought.

Her father exploded, "What is this? What do you two mean by embarrassing me like this? Girl, stand up right now!" Then he turned to her mother and demanded, "More wine—now!"

Marta tried to stand on her own, but her legs just wouldn't work. Saana's younger servant took her hand and helped her to her feet. Then with some difficulty, she stood up, still being lightheaded, she felt as if she were going to pass out again. Her hands were shaking, and her knees wobbled, beads of sweat formed across her forehead again, and her mouth was as dry as dust.

"Girl, come here—now!" her father shouted.

She walked over to her father in a semi-drunken fashion. She could barely keep her feet under her. Marta heard her father's voice as though he was talking in a tunnel.

Visibly furious with a face red with rage, her father graveled, "Marta, you will be married to Saana in four months' time, and I don't want to hear another word about it. Do you understand? He is to be your husband, and you will be thankful. Do you understand? Well, speak up, girl."

Her mouth was so dry she was barely able to squeak out the words: "Yes, Father."

Akeem continued, "Saana is a wealthy man, and your marriage to him will help our family tremendously, so be happy that you are able to do something good for your family instead of playing around all day like a child."

Her father showed no empathy or pity in his voice. Neither Marta nor her mother knew the inner torment Akeem was going through as well. No matter how concerned he was for his daughter, he felt he was between a rock and a hard place. Now that the deal was made, that was all there was to it. There was no going back, and in that, no more pleasant daydreams for his daughter as far as he could see— only nightmares; and he was truly sad about this.

Her mother was finally able to stand and started to open her mouth to plead with her husband, but with one vicious look, her husband stopped anything Sonta would have said. He had never struck her in their seventeen years of marriage, but she just knew that it would now come with a vengeance if she said a word. So she poured more wine and breathed a sigh of relief when she didn't spill any.

The girl looked at her mother and pleaded with her eyes. "Say something— say anything. Please help me! Oh, this can't be happening! Please help me!"

When Marta saw the tears running down her mother's cheeks, she knew there was no hope of rescue—no hope of living out her dreams. At that moment, she closed her eyes, took a deep breath, and decided that no matter what she would live strong. She determined that Saana was not going to break her as he had his servants. She was determined that—live or die—she would not be broken.

She thought to herself, *I will never break and become his slave. I will be his wife because I must, but I will die before I become his slave. What's the worst he can do to me? Kill me? Nat's not much of a threat if I consider myself dead already. How does one kill a dead person?*

Her mind was set, and in her resolution, she found new strength. Se dizziness faded, and a determined spirit buoyed her to a place she had never been before—life or death didn't matter.

She repeated to herself, "I am a woman and will be his wife but never his slave."

Each time she repeated it to herself she found that the feelings of despair would dissipate just a little more. Before long, she was consumed by a peaceful resolve that replaced her shock and disappointment. Her joy had left her; her dreams were gone. Nonetheless, an almost supernatural courage encompassed her.

Under her breath, she chanted, "If I can't be happy, then at least I can be strong."

At that point, to reinforce her decision, she turned and looked Saana directly in the eyes and asked if he needed more bread. It was a violation of custom in those days for a woman to look a man directly in the eyes, and her look caught him off guard. He let the moment pass as a social lapse by a teenage girl, but little did he know, he was looking into the future.

2
The Prince and the Peasant

Marta had a special place she would regularly visit that was outside the city walls near a stream under the canopy of several ancient olive trees and one huge willow tree. The stream made a wide bend at the foot of the huge willow tree, and on warm days like this day, she would bathe her feet in the cool water. This was her quiet retreat when she needed to get away from the pandemonium of her house, where she could think and dream in peace. Today, her courage was being challenged as never before with the announcement of the "arrangement," and she needed to gather her thoughts.

She lamented, "Four months! Four months and I will be married to that wretched man. Four months and I will be like a dead woman, only with my eyes wide open. By the gods, there must be some way to escape this evil fate. I can't run away. There is nowhere to go. What can I do?"

She sat with her feet in the stream for nearly an hour, pondering her fate when she heard a voice behind her, "Beautiful place, isn't it? I come here often to be alone in my own thoughts as well."

Marta was startled and spun around to see who was talking. Standing about ten feet away, next to the trunk of the willow tree was a young man about her age dressed in blue and purple clothing and had a blue silk turban on his head. A full head taller than her with a medium build, she observed that this young handsome stranger sported the beginnings of a thin beard. As she was scrutinizing him, she suddenly realized his apparel revealed that it was the attire of royalty.

She stammered, "My, my, my apologies, sire. I…I didn't realize that this was anyone else's special place. I've been coming here since I was a little girl. This is where I come to think and to be alone, where I can daydream out loud. Sometimes I come here just to get away from other people. It's my special quiet place. I will leave now. I come here often but didn't realize that I was trespassing. Please forgive me." She recognized that she was talking too much and scrambled to stand up.

The young man laughed and said, "No, no, you are just fine. Stay. You can stay. Just please don't tell anyone else about this place or that you saw me here. There is no place like it in the whole region. I come here when the palace is full of noise and when there are overwhelming demands on my time. Sometimes I just come here to escape." Looking down he said, "Sometimes I just need to get away." Then looking up, he added, "Today I received some troubling news, and I came here to think, to come to my special hideaway for a while. I just found out that I have been betrothed to a girl from a noble family from a city in Philistia. I have not met her. As a matter of fact, the first time I will meet her is at the wedding ceremony." The young man frowned, shook his head, looked down again, and said, "Oh, you wouldn't understand. How could you?"

Marta, downcast, bowed her head, trying to stop her own flow of tears, took a deep breath, and said, "I understand only too well. I just found out today that I have been betrothed to a man three times my age. His name is Saana. He is a rich farmer whom I detest. He is old, ugly, mean, and cruel. The wedding is scheduled to take place in four months. I feel like I have been sentenced to die, and Saana's house will be my hell. I would run away, but there is nowhere to go." She looked up with unchecked tears running down her cheeks. "So you see, I do understand only too well."

"Saana! Oh, you poor girl! I have met the man only once about a year ago and found him completely despicable. My father hates the man but says he pays more taxes than anyone else in the kingdom, so my father tolerates him."

The young man looked at Marta with sympathetic smile. "I feel your situation is much worse than mine. You know what you are marrying into, and you know it is bad. I, on the other hand, haven't any idea what this girl I am betrothed to is like. Is she spoiled? Almost undoubtedly. Is she pretty? Probably. All else is a mystery to me."

The young man walked to a place next to Marta and sat on the ground, pulled his sandals off, and put his feet in the water next to hers. "What is your name?"

"Marta. My father's name is Akeem, and he is a linen and flax merchant. We live near the west gate just inside the city wall. I have a mother and two younger brothers."

The youthful man cocked his head to the side a little, smiled, and proclaimed with a loud voice. "My name Jahailaman, son of Jorim king of Shunem, and I am sixteen and the only son of the king, and that means I am the future king of Shunem. Those who know me best call me Jal, and so can you." His voice got quieter, and his face a bit sad as he went on saying, "I have no brothers, no sisters, and I have no friends to speak of." He started to smile again. "And of course, I live in the great big palace, a truly magnificent home."

Again, his face became sad as he continued, "The palace is large and my father so busy I rarely see him, except at supper with about twenty other people surrounding him. My mother is in poor health, and she, for the most part, stays in her room—I don't see her that much. A prince's life, so you see, is not as good a life as one would suppose."

He smiled again and looked at Marta and asked, "What is your house like?

What is your family like? I don't have the privilege of leaving the palace often, and even when I do, I usually have to sneak out like now. Do you see your father a lot? What's it like to be able to come and go from your house whenever you want?"

He laughed. "I have so many questions, so many things I want to do. Just to talk to someone without having to watch every word I say is a pleasure. I'm not allowed to have many boys my age over to visit, so consequently, I have no real friends. My guardian is overly protective. He says, 'You never know when an assassin might try to get at your father through you. You are not an everyday child, you know, and we shall protect you.' He is mean, and I hate him."

Marta pondered Jal's questions and statements and felt compassion for him in his situation. Here he is a prince and lives like a prisoner. She was seeing the other side of the life of royalty few ever consider.

With a sigh, she uttered, "I want to thank you. I've had dreams of what it would be like to be a princess." Gazing up, she fantasized, "In my daydreams, I'm waited on hand and foot and bidding people, 'You do this, or you do that,' and they obey." With a change of tone, she continued, "I'm appreciating now that in many ways my life, though meager, is a much easier life."

She smiled and went on to say, "I live in a nice house not nearly as big as your palace. Our house has a ten-foot-high wall around it to keep bandits out. My father worries about the family and the possibility of bandits getting to us at night." She took a deep breath. "Also, I have two younger brothers whom I love, but they can be pests at times. It's hard to come here often because we are so busy. But I come here as often as I can—probably three or four times a week on a good week, but most times, just once or twice a week. What about you? How often do you come here?"

The two of them sat for over an hour talking, laughing, and were developing a close friendship when they were interrupted by a loud, booming voice, "There you are! What do you think you are doing out of the palace? We have been looking for you everywhere! Quickly, I need you to come with me. This is inexcusable! Your father will hear about this. I will make sure of it!"

Marta and Jal jumped up and were both unnerved by the sudden interruption. There stood a rather short, obese man, bald, with fat cheeks and a red face. He was just a little taller than Marta. The prince tried to reply but just stammered, wide-eyed and obviously terrified. Marta was confused, especially because the man was so demeaning to the prince.

Immediately, the prince got up and walked over to the man, and looking down, he apologized profusely. The man shouted, "Enough, now follow me." And they went back into the city.

Marta was incensed. She was determined to find out who this man was and how he could talk to the prince in such a terrible fashion. He was her friend now, and she was protective of her friends.

The next morning, she went to her special place, and the prince was already there. He was sitting by the stream with his feet in the water. He looked very depressed, and it appeared he had been crying. In order not to embarrass him because of his tears, she made a noise in the brush, knowing that this would give him some time to compose himself before she walked up to him.

"Good morning," she said with a large smile. "I'm so happy to see you again."

"Good morning," Jal responded, wiping his eyes, still trying to recover. He smiled, but she could tell it was a halfhearted response and that he was struggling.

Sitting down next to him, she took a deep breath and asked, "I must know. Who was that foul man that was so rude to you yesterday? I really didn't like the way he talked to you. Here you are the son of the king and going to be the future king, and this man talks to you like that. Who can he be that he has that kind of liberty?"

Jal responded, "He is my guardian, and my father has given him charge over me. He is always like that. I really don't like the man either, but I don't have achoice." Jal's smile faded, and he looked down and sighed deeply. "You need to understand. I don't have a choice."

Agitated, Marta stood up, walked back and forth, and boldly said, "I'm sorry, but I don't believe that. You are sixteen and a prince. I really don't believe your father knows about how this man treats you. I was shocked at his terrible behavior and even more shocked when you didn't stand up to him. Apparently, he has been your guardian since your early childhood. Am I right?" The prince nodded. "Maybe when you were around ve years old, he had some additional liberties to keep you safe and out of trouble but certainly not now. I consider you my friend, and I hate to see my friends abused. Especially when they are as special as you."

"I'm not so special," Jal said dejectedly. "As for why I responded out of fear, you would have to go through the abuse and the torment from the time you were a little child to understand. Fighting back has never been an option, and I stopped hoping a long time ago and have never had a real chance to fight back. From the time I was a small child, say three or four, and because of my mother's illness, she could no longer care for me. It was then that I became subject to this man's abuse, and my father never seemed to care, or at least it didn't appear so. You don't know what's it's like to be afraid to get out of bed in the morning but then be terrified of being found in your bed instead of being up and dressed. You can't know what it's like to be terrified of every sound at night. Afraid of not eating the right way or not doing well in your lessons, knowing that not doing something well brings pain, punishment, and abuse."

Jal continued, "My father is so busy that when I'm allowed to speak to him, it is rushed, and it feels like he never listens. I watch my father from a distance, and I am proud of him, but we never really talk. I am scared to complain to him about my guardian's abuses. What if he just sends me back to the guardian? Do you see my nightmare?"

Jal dropped his head and continued, "My mother has been sick for as long as I can remember. I seldom see her, and when I do, it is only for a few minutes and the guardian is always there. So there is no help from her. I have no one I can turn to. The guardian has friends throughout the palace, and they watch out for him, and he watches out for them, and they all watch me to make sure I'm obedient."

Jal kicked the water and said, "The guardian literally runs my life, and his friends monitor everything I say and do. What I say, what I eat, who I see, they watch everything. I've had thoughts of running away, but where would I go? When someone would find out who I am, I would be returned and subjected to terrible retributions. This place is my only escape. Besides coming here, I am trapped with nowhere to run. It's hard to have hope that things will get better. So you see, I am not really that special."

Marta responded with a quiet but firm voice, "Stop saying that. Yes, you are special. Remember you are going to be king one day and that already makes you special. You are talented and strong— you just don't know how much yet. It's time for you to stand up and be a prince, not just in title but in personality. When you walk into a room full of people, they all need to be at least a little intimidated. You represent power and authority. You are the son of the king."

She dropped to her knees next to him and looked him in the eyes and said, "Repeat after me, I am the son of the king."

Jal looked a little shocked and timidly stammered the words, "I…I am the son of the king."

"No!" Marta bellowed as she jumped to her feet almost forgetting who she was talking to—she never was easily intimidated.

This time, she was shouting at the top of her lungs. "Say, I am the son of the king! Say it with authority and power. Say it like it really means something to you."

The prince, with a look of realization covering his face, thundered, "I am the son of the king!" Then repeated it even louder, "I am the son of the king!"

Dropping back to her knees and reverting to a quiet voice, she said, "What does it mean to you to *be* a prince? Is it just a title? Or is it who you are? Is it what you are?"

Jal paused a moment and said, "I honestly have not thought of it. I have never had the title explained to me. I truly have no understanding of it, and I don't know how to answer your question."

Sitting down again, Marta put her feet in the water next to his and said, "To me, being a prince means the country looks to you for justice, for leadership, for hope when times are bad, and direction when disasters happen. That's what a prince is. For you to tolerate disrespect weakens you, and your people then lose a sense of justice, direction, and hope. We need you to be strong. We all need you to remember who you are. You must go straight to your father and let him know what has been going on. Be bold, be insistent. I really believe he doesn't know what's been going on. The guardian may have friends, but you have your father, go to him. Trust him, and trust yourself."

Just then, same as the day before, there was a shout from behind them that startled them both. "Again! Here again! What am I going to do with you? Get over here right now! We will deal with this when we return to the palace. I said get over here now!"

Just as the day before, Jal started to stand up. He had a tormented look on his face. Marta jumped up first and was furious. She turned and faced the man with her fists on her hips and demanded, shouting back, "Who is this peasant that talks to the prince in such a disrespectful manner?" Her blood was boiling. "This is the prince of Shunem and its future king, and you dare to raise your voice to him. May I remind you that this prince will someday be king, and on that day, he will not suddenly lose his memory. On that day, he will remember this day, when a servant embarrassed him in front of peasant girl, treating him as though he were low-level servant himself, like a delinquent stable boy."

She turned to Jal and said, "If I were you, sire, I would definitely bring this whole incident up to your father the king and see what he thinks about his son being treated in such a disrespectful manner by one of his own servants in front of a peasant girl."

The man shouted back and said, "I am the prince's guardian, and if you dare utter one more word, I will have you whipped. Now, sire, I need you to come with me."

Again, he spoke as though he were talking to a child servant instead of a sixteen-year-old prince; this infuriated Marta all the more. She shouted at the top of her lungs, "You, sir, are the one that will be due for the whip! A servant has no business speaking to a prince in that manner. Even my servants would never speak to me in such a disrespectful manner!"

The man walked up to her and slapped her on the face and started to slap her again. Instantly and reflexively, the prince grabbed the man's hand, and in so doing, for the first time in his life, the prince realized he was much stronger than his guardian. This awareness was as shocking as it was enlightening; so he, in his resentment, squeezed hard on the man's arm.

The guardian stood there in shock. He was wincing from the pain of the prince's grip, and tears from the pain were forming in the man's eyes. The guardian raised his other hand as though he were going to strike the prince; but Jal, full of adrenaline and shaking with anger, shoved him to the ground.

Now it was the prince's turn to be red-faced with fury. He was in unknown territory. He was the intimidator rather than the intimidated. He was trying to regain his composure, but his anger and this revelation were overwhelming.

He screamed, "You would dare raise your hand to me? The lady is right. I will remember this moment for the rest of my life or at least until I have fully dealt with you personally. After that, I swear by the gods I will never think of you again. You are right, someone will tell my father about today's events and that someone will be me—today!"

The prince turned to Marta and said, "Thank you. I will be forever grateful for your courage. Hearing your words and seeing your bravery roused my soul. I have been mistreated by this man for so many years that I had forgotten who I was."

Then turning to the man, Jal said in a low, menacing tone of voice, "And he has obviously forgotten who he is to me. Yes, my father and I will have a long conversation when we return to the palace."

Jal stood tall and looked down at the man lying on the ground. "But before we do anything else, I want you to say something right now. Say, Jal is the son of the king! Say it now!" The guardian sat up and looked in shock. "I said, say it now!" the prince said in a low, menacing tone.

The guardian started to stand up, but the prince pushed him back down. "I said, say it now. Jal is the son of the king!"

The guardian mumbled something inaudible below his breath. Jal took a step and stood over the man and said, "I will give you one more chance before I consider you a traitor and inform my father as such. Now say it!"

The guardian looked at Marta and then at the prince and said in a muffled tone, "Jal is the son of the king."

"Louder!" Jal screamed. "I want the guards at the palace to hear you."

The man yelled, "Jal is the son of the king!"

"Say it again!" Jal demanded.

The guardian, in a rebellious fashion, looked Jal in the eye and said, "Jal is the son of the king!" Then he glared at Marta with absolute hatred.

Placing his fists on his hips, Jal stepped back and ordered, "Now, guardian, stand up and follow me. If you utter one more word before I have a talk with my father, I…I will have your tongue for dinner."

The prince turned and winked at Marta then walked up to her and spoke quietly with a little quiver in his voice, "I will never forget this day. Thank you again for your courage and for your inspiring words." Then he turned to the guardian and said, "Get behind me and follow me to the palace and stay with me until I speak with my father. And oh yes, it would give me great pleasure if one of your 'friends' tried to interfere, you would be the first to pay the price."

The guardian started to speak; but with one look from the prince and seeing his fists clutched, he shut his mouth, bowed his head, and followed in submission. But then again, while walking away, the man glared at Marta with that despicable hate-filled look and then continued to follow the prince. Marta was unmoved.

Marta's face was still stinging from the guardian's slap, but watching the prince take over and instantly change from the boy-prince to the man-prince made her heart swell. The thought of how close she had come to real trouble for her and her family never crossed her mind until later that day when she told her mother all that had occurred. Her mother was not happy—no, Sonta was not happy at all. She carefully explained all the repercussions that could have happened to her and her family. Upon the realization of the potential trouble she could have caused, Marta was indeed shaken—but unashamed as was typical for Marta.

Early the next week, Marta was feeling exceptionally disheartened, so she went to her favorite place, only to discover that the prince was already there sitting by the stream with his feet in the water, singing a song under his breath. He visited this spot several times in the past three days, hoping to run into her again. When he saw her, with a large smile on his face, he stood up beaming with joy.

Jal asked, with a mock frown and hands on hips, "Where have you been?"

Marta responded, "My father was getting ready to go on a business journey to Egypt, and I had to help get everything ready." She smiled. "Were you looking for me? I'm attered," she said a bit sarcastically.

Jal said, "Yes, I was looking for you. I wanted to tell you what happened when I returned to the palace." Naively missing the sarcasm, he explained, "To my great fortune, I caught my father when no one was around and let him know about all the mistreatment and abuse—he was shocked. He asked me why I didn't let him know sooner, then he wept when I told him about how hard it was to talk to him and about all the guardian's friends that interfered whenever I tried. The finish of it was, the guardian was sold as a slave to a Philistine farmer, but not before he was given forty lashes for daring to strike me. Several of his friends were sold into slavery as well, and the others were demoted to wash servants. Although the guardian had slapped me many times in the past, my father told me that if he had known, he would have never allowed it to happen. I had ignorantly assumed the guardian had my father's approval, so I never said anything. Ever since I was a young child, I endured abuse, slaps, insults, and humiliations, so much that I became terrified of the man and his friends. I can't tell you what it feels like to inch every time an adult approaches unexpectedly. It's getting better now. However, I still have occasional tendencies to flinch."

He took a deep breath and said, "It wasn't until you spoke to me that I became enlightened—and then watching you—a peasant girl—stand up to him. Here I am, a prince, and you showed more courage than I have ever known. It was then that I realized I wasn't going to put up with his abuse anymore. Then when he went to slap you again, I just reacted without thinking and it was right at that moment—I knew. I knew I was much stronger than he was. I knew I didn't have to tolerate the abuse ever again. From that point on, I stepped into another place. It was more than just a realization. It was a spiritual awakening. That day, I became a prince. Not in title only but in spirit as well. You…your defiance, your words about me and to me, changed my life in an instant and forever. I'm just beginning, but with friends and good advisors and especially with the help of my father, I plan to be the prince you described."

With tears welling up, Marta uttered, "I couldn't just stand by and say nothing. My mother explained the risk I took by what I said, and it shook me a little. But I would do it all over again just as I did that day. There are some things that no one should ever tolerate, even if it costs them their life."

They spent the rest of the day sitting by the stream in the shade of the trees and talked about their dreams and hopes. They talked about what faced each of them in the future and how they planned to handle it. The sun had set, and the evening was well spent by the time they both got home. As for Marta, it meant she had some explaining to do. However, for the prince coming home late had a totally different outcome. No one was there for him to dread. He experienced freedom—free to come and go as he pleased. Finally, he was free! The impulse to look over his shoulder with fear was still an intense feeling, but now no one was there to frighten him.

He lay in bed that night, relishing in his newfound freedom. He reflected on Marta's words about his position and responsibilities. Then it was long into the night before the prince finally fell asleep, and he slept very well indeed.

Over the next four months, Jal and Marta met several more times at their beautiful haven by the stream and became fast friends. Sadly, the meetings ended when Marta married Saana, and the prince married shortly afterward.

3

Gehazi

Gehazi's father called out to his sixteen-year-old son, "Gehazi, Gehazi, hurry up! I need you to come with me this morning. I have some important business to accomplish today, and I need you to be there." Gehazi came running up to his father and asked, "What business is it? You say it is important? What is it? How can I help? What do I have to do? Important business and you want me to come?"

His father smiled. It was so much like Gehazi to be excited about being a part of "something important." He was a smart boy but at times a little overexuberant.

His father was a full head taller than the average man of the time, large and muscular, he sported a gray, well-trimmed beard. His head was bald except for a ring of hair that circled his head. He was a tough businessman and a hard negotiator but a loving father and husband.

The father looked at Gehazi, smiled, then said, "Relax, son, I will tell you what you need to do once we get there." He knew keeping him in the dark would drive his son to derision, and he would have to tell him to hold his questions several times—and he did have to remind his son—several times. In mocked exaggeration, he said, "You'll see when we get there, son, just be patient and please be quite. You are giving me a headache."

As Gehazi and his father were approaching the city gate, the boy noticed there were several town elders sitting in the shade, talking.

They all stopped talking when they saw the young man and his father coming. They had serious looks on their faces and stared at Gehazi in a way that made him very uncomfortable. His father had a serious look as well, then he broke into a large smile. Gehazi was confused and thought, "Where are the wine vats? Where are the merchants? Why are the elders staring at me like this? Am I in trouble?"

His father, the wine maker, stopped in front of the men and greeted them in succession of importance, starting with the eldest and richest to the next richest and on down. When he was finished, he turned and looked at his son and said, "Come here next to me, son." Gehazi stepped forward timidly. Then his father put his hand on Gehazi's shoulder and faced the elders and said with a loud strong voice that startled the boy, "Thank you for coming to my son's very special day."

Now, Gehazi was thoroughly confused. "What special day? It's not my birthday. What's special about today?"

His father cleared his throat and went on to say, "This is my son in whom I am well pleased. He can now do business in my name. Whatever he promises is my promise, whatever he commits to is my commitment as well. My son has proven himself trustworthy, a hard worker and very competent in my wine business. Granted, he is young and still needs to learn a lot, but he is one of the best workers I have ever seen. I am proud of my son Gehazi. Gentlemen, I give you my son once the boy and now the man."

With the final statement, the elders all got to their feet and came and each patted Gehazi on the back and congratulated him. Each one also introduced themselves to him and said they were excited for him. Gehazi was stunned. is whole event caught him totally off guard. As the realization came to him about what had just happened, tears started to well up in his eyes. "I have just been declared to be a man!" he said to himself. He turned and looked at his father and said, "Today, you just declared me to be a man." His father looked at Gehazi with tears in his own eyes and gave the boy, now a man, a great big hug; and all the elders cheered.

*****

As the years passed, Gehazi worked beside his father intently watching and learning the business. His reputation for being astute in the business and shrewd in his transactions grew daily. His father was extremely proud of his young protégé.

Nine years had passed, Gehazi, now twenty-five years old, continued to work with his father in his wine business. He had four older brothers and three younger sisters, and because of that, his prospects of a rich future were dim. His oldest brother would inherit double what he would, and after the rest was divided between him and the rest of his brothers, he would inherit very little indeed. He would probably end up working for his oldest brother as a kind of junior partner of sorts. He loved his brother, but he hated the fact that his status would be a little better than a hired servant. A well-paid servant but still a servant. What galled him the most, though, was that he was so much better than his brother in the wine business, and in business in general.

Gehazi was half a head shorter than the average man, and a full head shorter than his brothers. He was thin but strong for his size. He had a square, chiseled chin. The young man wore his beard shorter than most other men, and it was always immaculately groomed. Being a little vain and somewhat obsessive about his appearance, he always dressed in his best clothes, investing a large portion of his income for new clothes. He was a bit of a dandy.

Gehazi was a hard worker and faithful to whatever task he was given. Not necessarily handsome, he had thin lips and thick, black, tightly curled hair. Though Gehazi loved his older brother, he was also jealous of him. He despised his own station in the family hierarchy. He vowed that at the first opportunity, he would leave his family home and make a better life for himself. But opportunities were few and far between for a person in his position. Nevertheless, Gehazi dreamed of one day being a business success on his own, and he was determined to live that dream.

He was on a delivery run, and when he came to Marta's house and as he drove the wagon into the yard, he was met by Marta's father, Akeem, who was smiling and excited and had an unusual spring in his step. He enthusiastically called to Gehazi, "Good morning, Gehazi! How are you this fine day?"

Gehazi was taken back. The man's usual greeting was gruff and short, and all conversations were business-oriented, no small talk. He had never seen Akeem smile, and today, he was smiling with a very toothy grin and greeting him like he was greeting the sun in the morning. "Gehazi, I have a rather large order for four months from now. I will need fifteen baths of wine. Seven of your finest wine and eight of your regular wine. We are going to have a wedding feast, and you and your family are invited. Can I count on you to be there?"

Gehazi answered, "Even if no one else in my family comes, I will be there, but I am sure my family will be delighted to attend. So who is your daughter betrothed to?"

"Saana. He offered a large sum of money for her hand, and I agreed. She is certainly a blessed girl," Marta's father responded with an almost gleeful sound in his voice. He sounded as though he had just made his best business deal ever. But in the back of his mind, Akeem was starting to have some reservations about the whole affair. His concern for his daughter's welfare was growing by the day.

After delivering the day's order to Akeem, Gehazi thought to himself, *Saana! Oh, how I feel so sorry for the girl. That Saana is a horrible man. He will kill her spirit. I have never been to a sadder home than Saana's. A big and beautiful house but a very sad house. The servants have the look of total defeat on their faces. I have never seen one of them smile, ever. Not one smile, from the youngest servant to the oldest. It is a dark house indeed...poor girl.*

Marta's father went back into his house half expecting to see sad faces, and he would have to scold them all for their ungratefulness. After all, the family would be richer than they ever imagined, and his daughter would be even richer. He rationalized that she would live in a luxurious house with many servants; what could be better? But instead of seeing the expected sad face on his daughter, Akeem saw a firm look and a determination in her look and manner that he had never seen before. With vigor, the girl was cleaning and helping with breakfast. There was no evidence of the little girl he had seen grow up. She was acting like a grown woman. He was starting to miss the little girl.

The mother, on the other hand, was not so poised. She looked as if she had been crying all night; her movements were stiff and slow. A bit irritated, he simply grunted, "Ungrateful," and went to the courtyard to wait for his morning meal. But still, he was amazed at his daughter's demeanor. Again, trying to rationalize his decision, he thought out loud, "While Saana is not the best material for a husband, what he can provide for her will make up for all that, she will see. She will be rich beyond any girl's dreams, she will see." Akeem, so busy having been relieved of his tremendous debt and because it clouded his vision, could not fully grasp the sacrifice his daughter would have to make—that is, until now.

While baking bread, Marta looked over at her mother, and the girl saw the state her mother was in and said, "I will be all right, Mother. I promise you I will be fine. You will see, this will all work out for the better. I will make it work."

Sonta looked at her daughter with sad eyes and asked, "How can you say that? He is a horrible man, and you would be better off if we gave you to the leather merchant. Though he is not rich, he is at least kind," she choked out. "Your father is always after the money, it's always the money." She slammed her hand on the table and started to break down and cry again.

"Stop that!" Marta said with a loud voice. "I am stronger than Saana is. I know it. I will be all right. I'm not afraid. He is a sour man, I know, but that only shows me where he is weak. I will take care of his house, and he will take care of the business and that is how we will live our lives. Someday, I will have sons, and because of his age, Saana will be the first to die, then my life will be as we both hoped it would be. Until then, I will be strong, and I need you to be strong too."

Sonta was shocked at the depth at which her daughter had thought this out. She is only sixteen, and here she is thinking like a woman twice her age. Sonta was amazed at this beautiful and unusually preceptive girl's response to her situation. She somehow knew that Marta would be all right. There would be a test of wills, and she knew that in that battle, her daughter would win. She not only believed it, she also knew it. She laughed at the thought of so many adults that had intellectual run-ins with this girl, only to walk away amazed. From the time Marta was six years old, it was difficult to win an argument with her daughter. The girl was never disrespectful but always knew how to sway a person with her clever and perceptive ways.

The next three and a half months went by fast. The prince and Marta's friendship and affection grew deeper as they met at least once a week at their secret place. The girl and her mother were so busy that they barely had time to think of the days passing by. The wedding was two weeks out, and everything was going as planned when Gehazi arrived with this week's wine and had some bad news. Speaking to Akeem, he said with trepidation, "I'm sorry to say this, but we are running short of wine. The grape harvest was very poor this year, and we may not have enough wine for your request. We will do our best to bring you all that you asked for."

"What!" Akeem shouted. "Two weeks until the wedding and you tell me this now! This is an outrage, and I will not stand for it! I don't care if you have to go to all the other cities in the region and buy it, but you will bring me exactly what I ordered, or I will go to the king! Do you understand?"

"Yes, sir, I understand, and I will relay your instructions to my father." Gehazi knew this would be the man's reaction and dreaded this moment, but the moment was now over, and his part was done. Now to pass the message on to his father who would be equally furious. But would have to comply with Akeem's demand. Not delivering on a commitment of this size would ruin his father's reputation and his business.

His father liked Gehazi's obsessive nature and knew he never had to worry when he was given a task. With his chest puffed out in pride, Gehazi's father would say to his family and other elders in the community, "Someday soon, I will give him a share of the family business." To say he was proud of his son would be an understatement. Somehow his son's station in the family hierarchy never seemed to have crossed his mind. His father's open admiration would, at times, spark some jealousy from his brothers.

Gehazi headed back into the city and relayed Akeem's message to his father and was met with the expected response. His father yelled, "What am I supposed to do? The whole region is suffering from this grape pestilence. I will get him what he asks, but it will cost him dearly. Son, go to all the surrounding towns and give whatever price they ask, and I will pass on the extra cost to that…that…that… idiot!" he said with bulging veins and a red face. "Remember to collect the price from him on delivery. Let him just try to make a fuss about the price in front of any of his guests," he uttered as he rubbed his chin in thought. He began to calm down with a wry smile growing on his face.

Over the next three days, Gehazi went to several towns and managed to find vats of fine wine that were so expensive the merchants were having a hard time selling them before they went sour. And despite his father's orders, he was able to bargain with them and was able to bring the price down some, but only if he bought all their stock at once. It was a bit more than he needed but gured that either he or his father would find a buyer for a fine wine at even at a higher price.

Walking on his way back to town, Gehazi passed by a man in a long brown robe and a long thick walking staff. The man looked Gehazi fully in the eyes in a way that made him squirm. It was as if he was reading Gehazi's soul. "Good day, sir," the man said in Hebrew and with a deep, powerful voice.

"Good day to you as well," Gehazi responded.

Shunem was in the region of Issachar, one of the twelve tribes of Israel and was near several Jewish cities with Nazareth being the closest, so learning Hebrew was essential to any merchant wanting to run a successful business.

"Do you know how far the city of Shunem is from here? I have some business there—tell me, if you don't mind." The man asked in a manner that felt more like a demeaning demand than a question. "It's an hour's walk straight down this road. I am from Shunem and would be honored to show you the way—if you don't mind." Making a point of how the man asked him for directions. The man had Gehazi's curiosity. He hadn't seen him before, and his manner and appearance were unusual, so much so that he knew he surely would have heard of this unique man if he had visited the city in the past. The man replied with an understanding smile. "Thank you, I welcome the company."

They walked silently for a while when Gehazi, out of uncomfortableness at the quiet, finally broke the silence, asking, "I perceive you are a Jew, what city do you come from? I'm eager to hear any new thing from strangers."

The man responded without looking at Gehazi, "I come from Mt. Carmel, a long two-day walk from here. I have several disciples that I train in the prophetic ways of my faith. What is your business that took you so far out of your city? Most people do not walk alone this far from their city because of robbers and wild animals."

Gehazi responded, "My father is a wine merchant, and I was buying wine for his business. None of my brothers were available to come with me." Then Gehazi asked, "If you don't mind my asking, what business brings you to Shunem?"

The tenor of the question was again not missed by the man. The man stopped walking and turned to face Gehazi and said, "I am looking for someone that Yahweh my God is leading me to." Then with a bit of sarcasm in his voice, the man asked, "Tell me, does your father sell good wine or just the ordinary kind? I have no use for anything but the best," he said with a mischievous smile, making a counter point, goading the young man.

"Only the best wine," Gehazi said somewhat defensively. "My father is very particular about what he buys and who he buys it from. We are having some difficulties right now because of a grape pestilence, so finding any wine is difficult, especially good wine. But we do have some exceptionally good wines on hand, and I just purchased more this morning."

The strange man said, "Good. Please take me to your father. I believe we may have some business to discuss about several things, and maybe even about some wine."

The way the man said it shook Gehazi. He thought to himself, *Who is this man? What business does he have here? Maybe he needs wine for his disciples. Maybe the drought is worse and more widespread than we know and forced this man had to walk a long way to nd the wine he needs but what other business would he have to discuss?" Several thoughts crossed his mind, but he only responded, "As you wish, it will be my pleasure."*

Gehazi thought about verbally fencing with the man again but kept silent the rest of the way. He had a lot of questions, but this mysterious man frightened him a little. It was obvious he was a man of authority, and there was a lot more to the man than he was telling. When they arrived at his house, Gehazi had a servant summon his father. When his father came to the door and the look on his face showed that he immediately recognized the man. It was a perplexing look of respect and fear at the same time.

"What has brought you to our house, Prophet?" the father asked with a cautious voice. "Is there a problem? Are you here for good or ill? Whatever you need is at your disposal." Gehazi was shocked. He had never seen his father with even a hint of fear on his face, but this man troubled his father a lot. Who is this man that could shake his father so?

The prophet smiled and said, "I am here for good, not ill."

His father turned to Gehazi and said, "Bring the prophet into the house and make him comfortable. Give him whatever he wants. Do you understand?"

Gehazi nodded his head and said to the prophet, "Come, I will have the servants bring you food and wine. Here is some water. I will have a servant wash the dust from your feet."

Gehazi turned to the head servant and snapped in an unusual command voice, "Bring water and make our guest welcome. Bring meat and bread and some of our nest wine and serve him immediately."

The servant escorted the prophet into the house. Gehazi, turning to his father with a somewhat perturbed tenor in his voice, asked, "Who is this man? I would think him a prince the way you responded to him, and he is dressed in such uncommon clothes. I have never seen a cloak like he is wearing. Who is he to us? I have never seen you react to anyone this way."

The father looked at him angrily and said, "Watch your tongue! Do not use that tone of voice with me! This man is the Hebrew prophet, Elisha. He is more powerful than a hundred princes. Even kings fear him. Whatever he says comes to pass, for good or for bad, it always comes to pass. It is said he can destroy whole cities with a word. So I'm telling you do not fail to please this man. This is not a casual request—this is a command. You just make sure everything this man needs he gets, do you understand?" The strength and the urgency of his father's response told Gehazi that his father was very much afraid of displeasing the man and that he should be afraid as well. The Gehazi responded, "I will make sure it happens as you command." Still feeling the sting of his father's rebuke.

Immediately, Gehazi went into the house, hoping that no one had already offended the man in some way. He found Elisha comfortably sitting with some pillows under him and eating some dates. He was obviously happy with the meal and motioned Gehazi to sit with him. "Your father has some excellent wine, and the food is delicious. Thank you for all your care for me," the prophet said with a wide smile that immediately put Gehazi at ease. "Now please call your father in. I have something of importance to say for both of you." Gehazi sent the head servant to get his father and wondered what the outcome of this man's visit would be. His father came in a bit cautiously. Elisha motioned him to sit with them.

Elisha announced, "I have a request, and it is my hope that you will agree."

Gehazi's father, with a skeptical look and a cautious tone responded, "I am listening."

Elisha leaned back and looked Gehazi's father directly in the eye. "I need a dependable assistant, and I have been praying that my God would direct me to one. He sent me to the road I was on today, and there I met your son. My God told me that I would meet a merchant's son and that he would be the only one traveling on the road alone. Gehazi was that person. I came to you to ask that he be my assistant, with your approval of course. Would you approve? Of course, it would mean he would have to come with me to Mt. Carmel and wherever else my God takes me. I need to know today because I have urgent business, and I must on my way tomorrow morning."

This caught both Shunammite men by surprise. The father supposed the prophet wanted some wine or had some other request, but this request caught him totally off guard. The father stammered a second and then stopped and looked down in contemplation. He thought to himself, *What an opportunity, not only for my son but for the whole family as well. From what I hear, Elisha goes freely in and out of the courts of kings. I also hear there is not a more powerful man in the whole world. I would lose my son as a merchant, but who knows what benefits this may present in the future.*

Finally, he answered, "Let me talk to my son, and we will let you know later this evening. Why don't we show you a room you can stay in for the night so you can relax before evening comes," he said firmly but with grace. He was now back to himself as some of the initial shock of having Elisha in his house had worn off.

Gehazi was dumbfounded—doubly dumbfounded. First, by the request itself, then by the fact his father didn't turn it down outright. He thought, *What is my father thinking? We have a business to take care of. I don't want to leave Shunem. I have my own plans, and I can't do that waiting hand and foot on this man. What is my father thinking? After Elisha left the room,* Gehazi turned to his father with a perplexed look.

"Are you really considering this man's offer? What about the business? What about the future of this house? I really do not want to leave Shunem. I really don't understand what you are thinking."

Hearing the distressed sound in his son's voice, the father responded with a calm but firm voice, the voice of strength his son had come to revere and respect. "Think, son. You would come before kings and nobles of all sorts. What better way to expand our business? The rich and the noble alike respect and even fear this man and anyone who walks with him as well. You don't have to stay with him forever, just a few years until I call you back, and I will call you back, don't worry about that. Also, consider all that you would learn about the Jews, their God, their markets, their customs, and their politics. Yes, I think this is a tremendous opportunity for both you and the family. I want you to take him up on his offer."

Gehazi looked at his father for a long time and started to see the wisdom in what he was saying. Now instead of shock and attempted refusal, he started to become anxious to tell the prophet what he and his father had decided.

The next morning, the father and mother assembled the servants and saw Gehazi off on a journey that would change not only their lives but also the lives of untold multitudes.

4
The Wedding

It was the day of her wedding, and Marta found it hard to get out of bed. It was the last time she would use this bed. It was the last time she would have breakfast with her mother. It was the last time for a lot of little things she had taken for granted in her day-to-day life. Her mother came into the room and sat on the side of the bed. She had a weak smile, and tears welling up in her eyes.

"Marta, Marta, oh, how I will miss you. You are the heart of my heart. I will never take another breath without thinking of you. I will miss you so—oh, how I will miss you." The tears started to stream. Marta responded with a tender smile, "I am not dying, Mother. We will see each other in the marketplace, and I am sure I will be able to visit from time to time. It will be all right, you will see. Come, help me get dressed in my wedding gown."

Though Marta was extremely frightened, almost to the point of panic, she would never let anyone see it though, especially not her mother. Her mother was almost at her breaking point now and would never survive if Marta let her mother know her true feelings. Marta looked up and saw her father standing at the door to her room. He had a strange look on his face, a look of sadness she had never seen before. He looked at his wife and, in a tender, quiet voice, said, "I need to talk to Marta privately. I will only be a few minutes." Marta's mother got up slowly and never looking up left the room. "Marta, I have a few things to say and a heartfelt apology to make. I will start with the apology." He smiled sheepishly. "Because as you well know, that's the hardest thing for me." Marta smiled back. He took a deep breath and continued, "I am sorry for sending you away with this man. I was in a desperate financial situation and out of a hard heart and desperation allowed this marriage to happen. I can't stop it now. It would financially ruin us. We would lose the house, we would all be forced to be his servants, and he would be able to take you for his wife anyway because you would be his servant and couldn't refuse." Her father started to tear up, something she had never seen before. She had never seen her father show a tender side in her life. He was always stalwart and sober. She had rarely seen him laugh and never seen him cry.

Marta started to speak, and her father raised his hand and said, "Let me finish before you speak. I so regret this marriage and sending you away with this horrible man. I used to think he was special because he was so rich, but after the last several weeks, I now see him as the monster he is." Her father took a deep breath and continued, "Having said all that, I want you to know that I will protect you. If he so much as lays a hand on you, he will pay and pay dearly. That is my promise to you. I can't stop the wedding, but I can prevent him from abusing you. This is my promise to you: As long as I live, as long as I have breath, he will never get away with abusing you. This is my word, and I never break my word."

Marta stood up and hugged her father, and he hugged her back—hard. She could not remember the last time her father had hugged her. He hugged her as though he didn't want to let go. With tears streaming down his cheeks, he kissed her forehead and turned and left the room. Her mother walked back in with a perplexed look on her face and asked, "What was that all about? In all our marriage, I have never seen your father with tears in his eyes."

Marta just looked at her mother and smiled. Sonta then proceeded to help her daughter into her wedding gown.

The guests started arriving days ago. Relatives from all the surrounding towns and regions came to see the legendary daughter get married. Akeem had found places for them to stay with neighbors and friends. He set up beds in his house as much of the house as could hold. He set up some tents just inside the wall surrounding the house. Marta was continually talked about among all her relatives. Her beauty, mental acuity, and her sharp wit were renowned among her friends and family. She was a legend among her relatives, they all loved and respected her.

Marta was dressed in a fine yellow linen gown with an ornate red and green linen scarf over her head. She wore gold bracelets, anklets, earrings, and a nose ring. As was their custom, she looked down without engaging anyone's eyes and stayed in an area reserved for her and her immediate family. Even as nervous as she was, she smiled a great deal to put on a show that would not bring shame to her family. Everyone there was watching her closely. Her marriage to Saana was almost scandalous. His age and his reputation for cruelty and especially his social crudeness was well known throughout the region. But he was best known for how rich he was. Some of her friends and family were pitying her, and some were a little jealous of the riches they assumed she would be surrounded with, making the mistaken thought that with financial riches comes a rich and happy life.

Saana arrived and, as usual, was in a foul mood. Akeem gave him a cup of wine, but Saana just wanted this whole ordeal over with. "I have work to do." He looked over at the bride and thought she was pretty but a little skinny for his taste. As was typical of his demeanor, he looked at the whole affair with a critical eye. There were too many people, not enough food or not the kind of food he liked. The wine was not to his liking, and he hated all the children running around, though in reality, all he saw was two well-behaved young boys following their parents.

"How do you like the wine?" asked Marta's father. Saana responded with a growl in his voice, "It's not the sort of stuff I would serve at an important function like this. But it'll have to do, I guess. When does the ceremony begin? I'd like to get this over with as soon as possible."

Akeem was not surprised at Saana's rudeness; he had known Saana most of his life, and he disliked the idea of this marriage more and more. He tried to think of a way out but couldn't find any.

Akeem was finally starting to recognize just how special Marta was. The excitement about the money and his financial rescue had worn off. He thought to himself, *What curse am I sending my daughter to? This man is the devil himself. How could I make such a cruel arrangement?* He dropped his head and sighed, "Oh well, the die was cast, and I can't back out now. If I did, my family and I would be ruined. I don't have the money to pay him back, and he would demand the money be returned immediately. He would take everything we owned and make my sons and daughter his servants. No matter what I do, now there's no way out of this 'arrangement.'"

Marta's father stood and stared at Saana for a few minutes with a look that made Saana uneasy, and then he leaned over to Saana and with a deadly serious tone in his voice said, "We have not discussed this, but I feel I need to say it now. Marta is my daughter and is loved by me, her mother, and all her relatives. Neither they nor I will stand by and see her mistreated. It would go very ill for you if she were harmed in any way. We will be watching. This is the last time I will say this, but now it is said, and in my words, it is sealed. Don't try me on this as this is not a threat but an earnest promise. I give you my word, and I always keep my word."

Saana was a little taken back but attributed Akeem's sudden display of bravado to the wine he had been drinking. Deep down inside, though, he knew that Akeem was serious and meant every word. He had been watching the family observe him, and it was a little unnerving. He didn't see a friendly face in the group. He just wanted this over with, for a lot of reasons but mainly to put some distance between him and this girl's relatives. Saana ignored the threat and snapped, "When do we start? I'm anxious to get this over with."

Marta's father responded to Saana, "The ceremony will start as soon as the last guest arrives. It is the king's son. A messenger came by and stated that the prince had heard about the wedding and would like to come as a friend of the bride, and I naturally invited him. I was more than a little surprised, I didn't know the prince even knew of my daughter's existence. So you see, since it is the king's son, Prince Jahailaman, we can't possibly start until he arrives."

Making Saana wait was extremely satisfying to Akeem; he looked down and smiled. He was expecting another rude response from Saana, but none came. No one, not even Saana, would dare say a negative statement about the king's son. "Well, let me know as soon as he gets here, if you don't mind," Saana responded sarcastically.

Just as Saana finished speaking, there was a blast from trumpets at the front gate, announcing the arrival of the prince. Jal arrived with some intentional pomp. He had two trumpeters to announce his arrival and with several servants and soldiers accompanying him. He slid off his horse, walked directly to Marta, and made a slight bow. Everyone one in the crowd took a deep breath in amazement. Marta smiled and made a full curtsy in return.

"I didn't know you were coming until my father told me," she said with tears starting to run down her cheeks. "You're coming helps so much, means so much, you can't imagine how much. You are my very best friend, and because of your presence here, a terrible day has been made the most special day of my life." Then she said with a sly smile, "Except for my sixteenth birthday, of course."

Jal laughed and said, "I could never miss the wedding of my best friend." Then with a mock sad face, he said in a whisper, "I'm sorry I missed your birthday, though, but if I had known you then, I would have been there with gifts, lots of gifts." They both laughed. The prince bowed again and then walked across the open courtyard and up to Akeem and Saana.

Turning first to Akeem, he smiled, bowed, and gave his congratulations; then with a serious face, he turned toward Saana and walked within a hands breath to Saana's face. Looking down on him, he said in a low tone that only Saana could hear, "Marta is my very best friend, and I want you to know that if anything unpleasant happens to her, it will go bad for that person who would hurt my friend." The prince leaned a little closer. "Very bad indeed." Then the prince walked over to a place reserved for him as an honored guest.

Marta's father was still trying to understand how the prince knew his daughter. Neither Sonta nor Marta had ever told him about Marta meeting the prince and their developing friendship. They thought he would never approve of these meetings, even as innocent as they were, in a private place, a "special place." Sonta decided she would explain everything to him later after the wedding.

Saana, on the other hand was shaken to his very core. *The prince threatened me. Who is this girl? What am I getting into? Well, I'm friends with the king, and he would intervene if the prince tried to carry out his threat.* Just then, as if reading Saana's mind, one of Jal's servants came over to Saana and said, "My master told me to pass a message on to you that his father, the king, loathes you so don't look for any help from him. He said his promise still stands." The servant then leaned forward and added, "I don't know why he said this, but I wouldn't cross him if I were you." The servant turned and went back to where the prince was sitting. Saana then noticed the prince was intently staring at him. The stare made Saana squirm. Saana just wanted this day to be over as soon as possible. When her father threatened him, he only halfheartedly believed him, but when the prince threatened him, he was shaken to his core.

Within an hour, the ceremony was over, and the feast was on. After a full day of the wedding festivities, Saana and his new bride were off to Saana's house with a crowd of well-wishers shouting blessings at them. Saana kept seeing in his mind the look on the prince's face and replaying the word he said. He knew that if the prince felt that way and if Akeem carried out his threats, he wouldn't be able to look for help from the authorities. He sat muttering to himself. Finally speaking out loud, he said, "Thank the gods that's over."

It was the first words he had spoken to Marta since they left her parents' house. They rode in an ornately decorated cart pulled by one well-decorated horse, with a necklace of owers and an ornate blanket on his back. Marta kept her gaze down and smiled and said, "Yes, my husband, it is a good thing to have behind us." She knew to speak little and not to argue with this rude and uncouth man, or at least not yet. *For now, stay quiet and stay away and everything will be okay,* she said to herself over and over. Marta resolved that she would do this until an opportunity presented itself or action was demanded. She would wait to put her plans into action, and she had lots of plans.

Saana looked at her and asked, "You are not one of those talkative children, are you? The last thing I need is a noisome child underfoot."

"No, sir. I keep to myself most of the time."

"Good. I like my peace and quiet. You just tend to the house and the servants and let me attend to my business, and we will get along just fine. Is that understood?"

"Yes, husband, I understand." They didn't speak for the rest of the way home.

*****

Saana's house was exceptionally large, but the outside was not well kept. Weeds and overgrown bushes were throughout the yard and along the wall of the house. The area around the house was littered with all sorts of junk, from broken farm equipment to broken pottery, and even a few animal bones scattered around. He thought it was frivolous to "beautify" a house; for him, it was "just a place to sleep and eat." Marta wondered where the servants were, but then she thought, *They are hiding. They are staying out of sight as much as possible. They were hiding from a monster. I will change that. I will be their good guardian, their hope.* A new sense of purpose rose up in her. She knew she may be risking her life at times, but she was determined that whether she lived or died, she was not going to live with fear, and neither were her servants.

She instantly started to take stock in what needed to be done to make the outside of this house a showplace. Se area around the house needs to be made clean and orderly—the inside of the house itself would be cleaned from top to bottom. She assumed she didn't even have to see the inside of the house to know how unkept it was.

Saana stopped the wagon, jumped off, and immediately went to the barn without saying a word, leaving Marta to find her own way. Marta, gathering her basket filled with clothes and keepsakes from home, approached the front door, then dragging the door open, she went in. She was pleasantly surprised when she saw that the inside of the house was well-kept. The rooms were clean and orderly, the furniture was a bit worn, but that was an easy fix. A servant came out from an area in the back of the house, and she instantly recognized him as the one who tried to comfort her when she fainted. He seemed pleased to see her with his big smile. "It's so good to see you again, my name is Lo," he said with a pleasant voice.

As she glanced around the room, taking it all in, she replied, "It's good to see you as well. Where are all the other servants?"

Lo answered, "They are all in the kitchen, waiting to see you but fearful to come out if the master was in the house as well." And with that said, he called out the other servants.

43

From that same direction came six other servants, four women, one man, and a young boy about ten years old. They all looked afraid but at the same time glad to see Marta. For a few seconds, they just stood staring at her, and then finally, the servant Lo broke the silence. "This is Marta, our master's new wife and the new mistress of this house. She is a fine person, and I believe you can trust her." He turned to Marta and said, "Now let me introduce everyone. Let us start with the man Gamal. He does a little bit of everything around here. He can fix or build almost anything. Then here we have Lamel. At ten, he is the youngest of us. He helps anyone that needs help, especially Gamal. Then we have Hadiza. She is the cook and handles the household finances. The master gives her very little to cover the household costs, like food and utensils, but she is very prudent when she goes to the marketplace with the meager amount she is given."

Marta glanced over at Hadiza and noticed a look of impatience as Lo continued, "Then there is Misam. She is Hadiza's assistant as well as her daughter. Here is Shaiel. She is Hadiza's younger daughter who also assists Hadiza and assists in cleaning the house." He then pointed to a teenage girl about Marta's age. "This is Michael, whose job it is to clean the house and take care of the master's bedchamber. So this is all the household servants. The master has many other servants that work with him in the fields. And as for me, my name is Lo, I am an Egyptian and was sold to the master, it was said, for disappointing my prior master with my teaching. That is what Saana told me anyway. I personally think he bought me for a large sum of money so I could teach him the art of writing and speech, but he has never taken the time for me to teach him. I think it is out of pride and procrastination."

Marta looked at all their faces intently. She has always been able to measure people up quickly and accurately. By the look on her face, she saw some potential trouble in Hadiza. She could see that Hadiza was used to being in charge and had taken offence at a newcomer taking over. She was probably in her late thirties, shorter than Marta, a bit overweight with a round face, and flecks of gray in her hair. She wore a gray shawl over her head. The new mistress realized that she had to figure out a way to keep Hadiza in charge of her area and still manage the house herself. She thought, *I may only be sixteen, but I am now the head of this house and in time all of them will understand that—including Saana.* She looked at all of them again and then around the kitchen and said, "It is good to meet all of you. I hope you will be patient with me as I learn how things are done in this house. If you could show me my room, please, and then I would like to sit down with you, Hadiza, and get to know you."

Michael said excitedly, "I will show you to your room" and then proceeded down a long hallway to a room at the end. Marta noticed that Hadiza didn't follow them and was not surprised. The door was opened, and Marta gazed with amazement into a large room. She saw an abundance of multicolored pillows decorating the wooden plank floor. A large bed in the center of the room, also adorned with colorful pillows, and these particularly captured her attention. Along the wall were three large windows that were framed wooden latticework with jasmine vines entwined in and around. Whiffs of pleasant jasmine fragrance infused the air. On one side of the room a table was set with two chairs and, on the other side, another table with chairs was nicely arranged. Cream-colored fabric gracefully draped the sides of the windows, and the same material veiled the bed in luxury. Compared to her small room in the family home, this was quite lavish for this sixteen-year-old girl.

With excitement in her voice, Michael said, "This is your room, mistress, I hope you like it. I worked all week getting it ready for you. Hadiza had managed to save some money out of the household budget for the materials for the curtains and pillows. Months ago, Gamal built the bed and the lattice for the windows. Lo found the jasmine vines and transplanted them here. Lo wanted the room to suit the stature of the lady of the house." Michael asked with a plea in her voice, "Do you like the room, mistress?"

Marta was misty-eyed and said, "Like it? I love this room! It is absolutely beautiful! You all did an incredible job! I will remember this moment for the rest of my life. I don't know how to thank you, but I will find a way. I must ask, though, where does my husband sleep? It's obviously not here. I can't imagine him liking this room at all."

Michael was beaming at Marta's words until she asked about Saana's room, then Michael became serious and had a sober look

on her face. "No," she responded, "he sleeps in a small room at the other end of the house across the courtyard. He has never seen this room, and I doubt he will ever come here. He pretty much stays out in the barns or in the fields. He comes in the main house only for his meals and to sleep."

Marta was relieved to hear the sleeping arrangements but was dreading the marital expectations of later that evening. She was only sixteen and was somewhat naive about life but not so much that she did not understand the expectations of a new wife. The thought sent chills through her. Marta turned to Michael and said, "Have Hadiza come to my room. Tell her it is extremely important."

Michael replied, "Yes, mistress," and headed down the hall at a quick trot. A few minutes later Hadiza stood at the entrance of the door and said, "Well, I am here. Is there something you wanted? Michael said it was important. It had better be. I have supper cooking." Marta was a little taken back by Hadiza's abrupt and disrespectful words but not completely surprised. Her mother warned her that this display of disrespect was probably going to happen, and she had rehearsed a response with her mother just in case it did. She knew she had to deal with this issue of respect and honor right now before anything else was done with the house or the staff.

"Is it my age that has you confused?" Marta said with a smile and a satirical singsong voice. "Or is it, perhaps, that I am new to the house, and this has thrown you off balance a bit?" Then Marta leaned forward and with a somber look and in a deeper but quieter voice said, "Or is it because you have been in charge so long that you have forgotten your manners and your place?" Marta walked over to Hadiza, who had a shocked look on her face and stood an arm's length from her, looked her straight in the eye, and continued, "Let me remind you of your place in this house. You oversee the household staff and the budget, and I oversee the house as well as the servants. If you want to remain in charge of the staff and the budget, then respect is in order. Otherwise, there are others who can do your job and the only thing you will oversee is my relief pot. Is that understood?"

Hadiza looked Marta straight in the eyes and started to say something then realized that this girl was not intimidated and was issuing a serious threat and was not bluffing. So thinking of a wiser response, she looked down and, with a much more contrite voice, added, "Yes, mistress."

Then Marta said with a firm but friendly voice, "Good. Now we will agree that this moment never happened and will never be spoken of again. Does that sound satisfactory to you?"

Hadiza said with a sigh of relief, "Yes, mistress," and looked up again.

Hadiza tried to convince herself that she was not afraid of this little girl, and she would not challenge her because she was terrified of Saana and has been at the business end of a few of his tirades. She rationalized that any bad report from this young upstart of a girl would not end well for her. Hadiza was no fool; she now knew that it was not wise to tangle with her new mistress. She was more intimidated by Marta than she liked to admit. The lines of authority had been clearly drawn and this young girl had drawn them—clearly.

Later that evening, Lo came to her room to let her know the evening meal was ready. Marta pulled a shawl over her head and came to the supper table where Saana was already sitting.

There were plates and bowls of food already in front of Saana, and when he saw Marta, he commanded, "Get me some wine."

Marta replied, "There are servants for that kind of thing. I came for my supper. Or is it that a mistress of the house has no more status than a servant? If the servant does not wait on you properly, I will deal with them. But make no mistake, I am not a servant, nor will I ever be." Then she sat down on the opposite side of the food from Saana.

Lo and Shaiel both took a sharp breath as they were serving, fully expecting their master's fiery explosion and the sure painful consequences the mistress was about to experience. Instead, Saana only grunted and yelled to Shaiel to get more wine. For Saana, it was just more than he wanted to deal with right now. He was tired and just wanted his supper. He really did not care who ran the house as long as he was not bothered with the details. He was taken by surprise, though; he hadn't expected her sudden defiance and her remarkable show of courage. There was a lot more to this girl than he realized. He also surmised correctly that she would die before she would bend. He liked her spirit if it didn't get out of hand, and if it did, he was confident he could handle her. He continued eating and didn't say another word.

After eating, Marta was dreading what would come next on the first night after the wedding. She was slow in getting up from the meal and went into the kitchen, both to talk to the servants and to hide from what she assumed was the inevitable wedding night expectation.

An hour passed by, and she was still in the kitchen and no word from Saana. She went into the main room of the house, and he was gone. She asked Lo where Saana was, and Lo told her that he went to his own bedroom to retire for the night. Marta had a feeling of overwhelming relief. At least she would not have to deal with that part of the marriage tonight. "I'll worry about that tomorrow when tomorrow comes," she said to herself with a deep sigh.

The next morning, Marta was awakened by the sound of Saana shouting at one of the field servants. She was not sure what the problem was and felt deep pity for the servant. She got out of bed and saw Michael standing next to one of the tables with a fresh bowl of water and with a towel beside it. Marta washed her face and, with the assistance of Michael, got dressed.

The loud shouting stopped, and the house was quiet. Too quiet. The servants were all afraid to make any noise at all. Saana was known to take a stick and wander around the house, intimidating the servants and occasionally striking them for some perceived infraction, real or not. They never knew when it was coming or many times why. Marta understood how dangerous her open rebuke of Saana was, but she had to stick with her plan. She would remember, though, to "try" to be a bit more cautious next time she stood against him but, at the same time, not to appear weak.

When Marta went into the kitchen to get some food, she was told by Misam that her breakfast was set out for her in the dining area. She reminded Misam of her rule that she would have her morning meals in the kitchen then instructed the servant to have her breakfast moved to the kitchen. The new mistress expressed that she wanted to talk to the staff while she ate her morning meal and would prefer to eat what they ate—with them. There was a sound that came from the direction of the kitchen doorway; it was Lo clearing his throat, looking confused and agitated.

Nervously reckoning, he said, "The mistress never eats with the servants— it's just not done." Lo, in a low voice, repeated, "It's just not done."

Marta responded, "Well, that's how it's done here from now on, understood? So bring my breakfast into the kitchen and have everyone gather there while I am eating, I want to speak to all of you. I have a lot of questions."

The look on Lo's face became more sober. "Yes, mistress." Straight away, he and Seeta moved Marta's food to a table in the kitchen.

The servants were already in the kitchen and had pensive looks on their faces when they saw Marta enter and sit at the table with them. When Marta saw the look on their faces, her heart was pricked almost to tears. Marta began with a soft, tender voice, "I am not Saana, and I am not at all like him. But though I am young, and I am not like Saana, I expect"—she then corrected herself—"no, I demand respect. I will never relay to the master any issues concerning the house. No, I will handle them personally, and make no mistake, I can and will handle them. Now that this is understood, you must know that I will never ever abuse anyone. I will work right alongside of you, if time permits, and I will always strive to be on your side."

She looked at their faces again and said with compassion, "I can see you have had more than enough ill treatment. I would have you call me by my name, but I fear Saana would react very badly to that level of familiarity. As far as I am concerned, we are a family, and we will treat each other as family. We have a lot to do to improve the appearance of this house, and we will do it together. Now with that said, are there any questions for me?" She looked around. "Go ahead and ask. I am serious about the part of us being a family. We must treat each other as though we were brother and sister, with me being the eldest sister."

Lo stood up, saying, "I have been a servant in other households. Though some were cordial and friendly, we were never considered family. It will take a bit of getting used to." The rest of them voiced their agreement that this was a strange but at the same time delightful turn of events.

Marta smiled and said, "I understand. So that part is settled, and now I have a lot of questions."

For the next two hours, Marta discovered a great deal—some of it good, but mostly, it consisted of stories of Saana's tirades and the unfortunate people he directed them toward. She assured them that she would defend them to the best of her ability—unless someone goes behind her back. She emphasized that she would still be that person's mistress, but he or she would be on their own —certainly not a good situation for the that person. When she finished asking questions, she asked Lamel to show her around the farm. Beaming with enthusiasm, he said, "Follow me. I would be glad to show you the farm and introduce you to some of the eld servants."

Lamel was tall for his age, and he was painfully thin. Marta thought to herself, *I must see to it that he gets more to eat. I will talk to Gamal since he works with Lamel all the time, he probably knows Lamel's situation best.* Dark-brown curly hair covered Lamel's head, and underneath, he had large, dark-brown eyes. He was highly energetic, with a continual habit of fidgeting.

The farm was huge, with hundreds of acres of pasture and farmland where herds of cattle grazed along with thousands of sheep. The field servants were busy with what seemed far too much work for so few hands. There was a stream that ran through the middle of the farm, which was rare in this part of the country. Several willow trees lined the banks of the stream. It was a beautiful sight to see.

She saw Saana about the same time he saw her. The look on his face was angry as he was obviously not happy seeing them there. He stormed over to them and yelled, "What are you doing here? Is there not enough to do at the house that you have time to take a lazy stroll and bother the men out here?"

Then looking at Lamel, he went to strike him across the face, and Marta jumped in between them. "He is my servant, and if you strike one of my servants, you will have to deal with me. If you strike me, you better not go to sleep at night, I promise, you will not wake up looking like the same man." She was initiating her first bluff and the most dangerous part of her plan for survival in this marriage—don't allow herself to be bullied.

Saana slapped her on the face and expected to see her act more contrite and drop her gaze; instead, she stood erect, stared him straight in the eye, and said, "That was a mistake on your part, and you will pay dearly." She was pitching her bluff—a dangerous bluff indeed.

He struck her again, and she didn't bend. She did not even inch, and the look in her eye made Saana uneasy. He thought to himself, *She wouldn't dare touch me even in my sleep, the consequences would be too great.* But the look in her eye led to him believe that this was probably a wrong assumption. This girl had a backbone, and the look on her face and the sound in her voice made him feel sure that this was no empty threat. He was going to bar his door that night just in case. What had he gotten himself into when he married this girl? No one had challenged him like this in many years, and that person paid a high price for his insolence. To stop her, he would have to beat her within an inch of dying, and then he would have to deal with her father and her other relatives who would be furious. Akeem would react out of honor, but the other relatives out of their love for the girl. Both would want revenge. Saana had so many enemies that he knew no one would come to his aid, especially not his servants. He could go to the king, but he knew the prince was right, that the king disliked him as much as anybody. The prince himself was another issue all together, and very much a bigger threat than Marta's father. He realized he had to defuse this issue right away, but not in front of the servants—that would make him look weak.

He turned to the servants and bellowed, "Leave now, or I will beat each one of you!" After they had all left, he tried a poorly devised pretense. "I could kill you right now, and there is nothing anyone could do about it."

She stared him straight in the eye and said, "Then do it. But don't think you won't suffer the consequences of striking me, if not from me then from my family for sure. Or I have a better idea. You can apologize to me in front of the staff." She knew he was bluffing, and she had put him in a corner with only one way out. His face was red with rage, but he knew he was in a no-win situation. He thought, *She was clever, oh yes, very clever.*

He growled at her. "You will pay, yes, you will pay. I will make sure of that." He whirled around and left muttering to himself on the way to the house.

A small wry smile came across Marta's lips as Saana stormed out. Undaunted, she followed him to the courtyard. She kept her eyes locked on him as he sat beneath a fig tree. He looked up and was startled to see that she had followed him there. He thought for sure she would be hiding somewhere. The look on her face frightened him, a strange feeling for a man that was used to being the intimidator. *This girl must be insane!* he thought to himself. Rage started to build in him again, and he stood up and started walking toward her. Unmoved, she continued walking toward him, her eyes locked on him the whole way. He stopped about six feet from her and screamed, "Are you crazy, girl? The only reason you're still alive right now is out of consideration for your family."

She responded with a slow, deliberate tone, "I understand that you are worried about my family, and you certainly should be. If you were to beat me or go as far as to kill me, my family would be seeking revenge. I estimate you wouldn't be a week before someone found you dead. Am I right or wrong? I can see by your lack of speech that I am right, and you already knew it. So we will never let this happen again, will we? From now on, you will stay at your end of the house and never bother me or the staff again, will you?" She smiled, and to accentuate her bluff, she said, "All men must sleep, especially a man that works as hard as you do. And as tired as hard workers get, they sleep deeply. If you ever want to sleep deeply again, this will never happen again, will it? Or your other option is to kill me. Which will it be?"

As soon as she learned she was to marry Saana, she determined she would die before she would ever allow herself to be battered. And she meant it. If this bluff would cost her life, then so be it. She asked, "Do we have an understanding?" never taking her eyes from his. He was flummoxed. How did he ever get into a position where a little girl could get the better of him? He had no option, no other way out. He knew deep inside that if he ever struck her again, she or her family or even the prince, would kill him or have him killed at the first opportunity, and there was nothing he could do about it. He broke the stare, looked down, and said, "Yes, we have an understanding." He suddenly felt more tired than he had ever felt in his life. He had been beaten at a game he was not accustomed to losing and he was a very poor loser.

Marta turned and walked away, taking a deep, shaky breath. *I thought I was a dead woman. By the gods, I thought he was going to kill me.* Trembling, she went to her room and collapsed on her bed.

$$\frac{5}{}$$
Lines Drawn

Life quickly evolved into a routine of getting up when the rooster crowed and working on the house until there was no light to work with. She and the staff were developing a deep familiarity and mutual respect. Their trust in one another was growing daily. Even Hadiza had started to develop a healthy respect for this unusual girl. Marta had shown herself as one of the bravest and smartest people she had ever known or even heard of. Marta had stood up to Saana, and she had never seen anyone do that before and not suffer extreme consequences, and yet somehow, this girl managed it. Marta demanded and got a larger household budget, and though it was not a tremendous increase, it was an increase. Hadiza remained in charge both the staff and the budget. Marta met with Hadiza regularly to review the budget and entrusted her with the day-to-day budget duties.

A healthy and respectful relationship started growing between Marta and Lo as they set a time each day for him to teach her to read and write. In their culture, this privilege was limited to men only, and even then, very few men were afforded this advantage. Lo was also teaching her eloquent speech, a tool she thought would be very useful in time. She found Lo to be brilliant, practical, and wise. Quite small-framed, though, for a man in his midthirties, about Marta's height with small hands. Not the hardworking type, probably would last only a day in laborious fieldwork. His hair was black and bushy, his skin was darker than the other servants, with an angular nose and a face that he kept clean-shaven. Overall, he was handsome in his own way.

Marta rarely saw Saana; if she needed to talk to him, she would hunt him down in the fields. She observed that he was a hard worker and didn't just supervise the field servants but worked with the animals and behind a plow just as often as his servants. His work ethic gained a grudging respect from Marta. When they did talk, he kept his part of the conversation short and to the point. He resented talking with her because she had beaten him at his own bullying game; she just couldn't be intimated by his nonsense, and this tormented his soul.

The house almost where Marta wanted it, clean and fully repaired inside and out. Gamal, the craftsman, made all sorts of furniture and completed a host of household repairs. Gamal was in his own little heaven. Lamel had pretty much adopted Gamal as a father figure and was learning how to use all sorts of tools. He was also receiving writing lessons from Lo and was learning quickly. Marta had encouraged Gamal about seeing to it that Lamel ate more, and it started to show. Lamel had been gaining some weight and looked healthier than ever.

She made sure that everyone pitched in with the house cleaning, and more and more she treated Michael as her daughter and handmaid. She found Michael to be highly intelligent but quiet and easily intimidated. Marta would work on her timidity when things settled down and the house was where she wanted it.

Hadiza's daughters, Misam and Shaiel, were typical teenage girls who quietly quarreled with each other but were hard workers and obedient to their mother.

The years went by uneventfully. The house was finally in order, and Saana was richer than ever. Her father's business was doing well, and she and her father had become closer than ever. It turned out her father was somewhat intimidated by his incredible, now adult daughter. Essentially, he was only comfortable in business and was awkward with close relationships. Trying to relate to Marta was especially difficult for him, but he was improving day by day.

Marta was able to visit her mother frequently, and she found her to be a world of wisdom. However, one issue made her hesitant about visiting, and it was the question of children. "When do you plan on having children?" her mother asked almost every time she saw her.

"There is plenty of time for that in the future," Marta would reply. But as the years went by, she started to think in the back of her mind, "I need to talk to Saana about this, but I dread it. He has never even touched me with any type of affection since the day we were married, and it is hard to imagine him doing so now." Their relationship was as distant as two strangers passing on a busy road.

Her family occasionally came by her house, but it was usually Marta that did the visiting at her parents' house. The thought of running into Saana kept most friends and relatives away, or if they did come, it was usually a very short visit. It was hard for Marta, but she had one consultation, her servants. Her servants that were more than servants; they had become her closest friends and, just as Marta hoped, more like family than friends.

As for Saana, his work was his friend. It was slowly dawning on him that his bitter attitude toward the world was alienating him from every person he knew. They would do business with him, but only reluctantly, and with suspicions about any possible wrong motives Saana might have. These realizations made him even more bitter. Se situation came to a huge conflict one day when Marta's father came for a visit and saw bruises on her cheek. He assumed that Saana had struck her and no manner of protest from his daughter could convince him that Saana didn't cause her bruises. Actually, it was an accident as she was struck by a bucket when she pulled it from a shelf and lost hold of it. Her father had come to dislike Saana so much over the years that he was just looking for an excuse, any excuse, to physically go after him.

He stormed out into the field where Saana was and roared, "How dare you strike my daughter. I warned you what would happen if you ever did." He proceeded to punch Saana in the face and chest. Marta jumped in between them and again explained how she got the bruise, and this time, her father listened to her but not before he had bloodied Saana's nose and cheek. Saana was furious and with his shrill voice threatened, "I'll take you to the elders and charge you for assaulting me!"

Akeem looked at him as he thought of the pathetic character Saana was and then said smugly, "No one would listen. You have made so many enemies that they would blame you, and I would be vindicated. Yes, people will buy your wheat and barley, but your character is so unredeemable that no one will have anything to do with you personally. I feel sorry for you." The words "I feel sorry for you" stung Saana more than anything else that had happened. He was furious and took a swing at Akeem but missed. He swung so hard that when he missed, he fell to the ground, and this only added to his humiliation.

"Get off my land before I sic the dogs on you." Actually, he had no dogs, but in his rage, it was the only vengeance he could conjure up at the time. His servants just stood by and watched.

Akeem turned and walked back to the house with Marta close behind. When they got to the house, Marta said, "I told you he didn't hit me, he wouldn't dare."

Her father responded, "Now he will be doubly reluctant to strike you. He might yell, but I don't think he will ever hit you. I must leave now. I have to go to Jerusalem to sell some cotton cloth, and I won't be back for ten days. I just wanted to make sure you would be all right." He left her house and headed home.

The last statement caught Marta off guard. Her father had seldom shown affection toward her and had never acted like he worried about her. It felt good—really good. For the first time in her life, she felt as though she and her father had a truly loving relationship. She had no idea how Saana was going to react to her father's attack, but she knew no matter what she could handle it.

After her father left, Saana stormed into the house and went straight to Marta and demanded, "What was that all about? Why did he strike me?"

Marta responded, "He thought that you were the one that bruised my face. He was wrong, and I told him so, but he hates you so much that he would not listen. I shiver to think of what he would do if you really did strike me, I believe it would be very bad for you. But then we have had that discussion before, haven't we?" She turned and walked away. Saana took stock in what she said and resolved he would have nothing to do with her at all to prevent any future "misunderstandings." Yes, they were married, but that was as far as their relationship would go if he had anything to say about it.

He thought, *She has been nothing but trouble since she came to this house. Granted, the house has never looked better and the food has improved dramatically, but I feel no one in the house takes me seriously. They do not fear me anymore. I should wade through the house and beat every one of them just to reinstill that fear again."* He knew he would never be able to do that; Marta would intervene, and he was sure she would follow through on her threat to come in at night and deliver her own form of punishment. In his estimation, Marta was a woman who made no empty threats, and because of this, he had come to fear her. She had him inching at shadows.

Saana left the house and went to one of the barns and proceeded to drink as much wine as he could before supper. Within an hour, he was drunk, and in another hour, he was passed out in the barn. When he finally woke up, it was late in the morning the next day.

6

A Heartbreaking Promise

More years passed, and Saana was now nearly sixty. Marta was now twenty-six and still childless—Saana had never consummated the marriage even after all these years. Marta was now getting concerned. "How do I correct this situation? I'm afraid Saana is so bitter that he will never give me a child." For Saana, it was his way of getting revenge; it was his way of getting the last word.

Saana would grumble to himself, "They may threaten me for touching 'that woman,'" as he had come to call her, "but they can't do anything to me for not touching her. She will die childless as far as I'm concerned. I don't care if some enemy of mine takes the land, at least she won't get it. Oh, how I hate that woman." Saana was consumed with hatred toward her and blamed her for no one liking him. It was easier to blame her than to look at himself. He imagined and plotted evil plans for her destruction, but he could nd no way to carry them out without the end result being dreadful for him. Her family and friends—especially the prince—would extract their full price of revenge on him. Above all things, he wanted to live.

Marta's mother didn't know about the lack of intimacy between them; she just assumed that it was just not the timing of the gods. When Marta would come to her family home, she would be met by some well-meaning friend who would foretell, "Se gods are going to give you a child by this next summer or by winter." This happened over and over again, and it hurt just a little more with each successive declaration. Her friends and relatives would give her all kinds of advice on how this poultice or that potion would work. She kept the truth to herself, but the dream of having a child just grew to a point that it was becoming overwhelmingly painful. She tried to put it out of her mind, but it became doubly painful when her brothers started having children.

Hadiza, who by now had become Marta's most faithful friend, saw the torment that she was going through. She tried to encourage her by saying, "Maybe he will die, and you can then remarry." Both knew that even if he did die, the prospects of remarriage was slim. Saana had no brothers, and few if any men would marry a twenty-six-year-old woman that had been married to Saana, even if she was a rich woman. His name was like poison.

One evening, Saana had gotten very drunk, and in the middle of the night, he had worked himself into a drunken rage. He headed toward the house with one target in mind, Marta. He burst into her room in an angry rant, slapping her and forcing himself on her. Afterward, as bad as the incident was, she had this one thing she could hope for, maybe she got pregnant. It gave her the strength to get past the ugliness of it all. She let Hadiza know of the incident, and both prayed for a miracle.

The weeks went by, and she was late in her cycle and hope started to rise in her heart. *Maybe, just maybe, oh just maybe!* She told Hadiza, and they hugged. They were going to tell the others the next day, but that night, her cycle came. Marta was crushed. Now the reality and the pain and the humiliation of the assault was like a mountain falling on her. In her room, while all alone, she wept. Not just a sniffle kind of crying, but a deep sobbing rose up from her soul. Devastated, the next morning she went to Hadiza and let her know, and they both cried. Hadiza hugged her and tried to console her, but she couldn't come up with words that would make Marta feel better, so she just held her and wept with her.

Two months later, the same thing happened; again, Saana was drunk and burst into her room, telling her how much he hated her and forced himself on her again. Sis time, though, she put up no resistance because of the faint glimmer of hope that still stirred in her. She wanted to fight, to make him pay for his cruelty, but the hope of having a baby overcame her thoughts of revenge.

Again, a couple of weeks went by, and her cycle came. This scenario was happening more and more frequently and always with the same result. Slowly, Marta's ability to hope was dying. She never resisted because of the hope that even in his cruelty Saana may give her the one desire of her heart, a baby, but to no avail. Now she had stopped fighting out of a sense of hopelessness.

Repeatedly, well-meaning people would ask her the question, "Are you with child?" Or say, "You look like you have a mother's glow about you." Or worse yet, "I have a word from the gods that you are going to be pregnant before the end of the month." Or even more disheartening, "The gods told me you will hold a child by spring or summer." The friendly diviners covered all the seasons, recommended a variety of potions, and various other possible ways to become pregnant such as waiting for the new moon, full moon, sundown, sunup, and on and on. Each time, Marta would have an ember of hope fanned into life only to be snatched away. No matter how bad it hurt, hope would rise again in her, only to be crushed with the advent of each monthly cycle. The pain was unbearable and getting worse. She became reluctant to go to her family's house for fear of someone bringing up the question of when she planned to have a child. Her spirit was slowly breaking. Saana's revenge was cold, terrible, and as complete as revenge could possibly be. If he meant to torment her, he found the perfect tool to do so.

Another couple of years went by, and still no baby. In the quiet of the night, when things came to a halt and the house was still, she was continually denied sleep by her torment. It never totally went away—it was a gnawing pain that just wouldn't stop. She kept up a stoic front so one would never know the torment she was in. She hid it in her work and in her conversations. She was good at covering up her own emotions and deflecting questions about how she was doing. Her mother asked many times because she knew something was wrong, but Marta was good at avoiding questions or at least avoiding answering them.

It was at this time that she noticed a mysterious man making visits to the city with Gehazi at his side. This must be the man they were talking about who hired Gehazi away from his father. Looking at Gehazi, she detected that his countenance had changed—his look exuded confidence. The man he served was a full head taller than

Gehazi and far broader across the shoulders. He had straight, black hair that touched the base of his neck and a beard that had grown down to his chest. His bushy eyebrows and dark, piercing eyes accentuated his intense look. Weather-worn and leathery, this man appeared to be one with a sober personality. His large, calloused hands curled around a thick walking staff. The long, brown cloak he wore conveyed a mysterious and commanding manner. He obviously was no ordinary man; by the way he conducted himself, you could see he possessed authority. She hadn't heard much about the man other than he was a Hebrew from somewhere north of Shunem. She would see him travel on the main road that passed by her house.

On one hot summer day, she saw him and Gehazi approaching at a distance through the waves of arid air. An overpowering urge to invite him to dine at her house suddenly seized her. She walked out of her house and did something that was not acceptable by a woman of that day, as she saw him walking down the road toward her house, she called out to him—a stranger. He kept walking as if he didn't hear her. She called out again only louder, and still, he ignoredher. When it looked as if he would just walk past her house and not acknowledge her at all, she began to fear that she would miss her chance to meet this extraordinary man. For some unknown reason, she just felt compelled to learn of him. Then again, out of sheer desperation, and against all present-day protocol, she ran out and grabbed his arm and pleaded with him to come and dine at her house. The look on the man's face was not of surprise or even annoyance but was almost as if he expected her actions.

Gehazi was aghast. "Marta, what are you doing? Have you lost your mind?" She looked at Gehazi with a pleading look and said, "Please ask him to follow me and have supper at my house." Gehazi shrugged his shoulders and complied, and the man agreed. As they began heading toward Marta's house, she shouted to Hadiza, "Please have two meals prepared for some unexpected guests." Marta escorted Elisha to the house holding his arm the entire way as if she was fearful that he was going to get away. They came into the house, and Lo already had the ceremonial bowl for foot washing ready; and Misam, Hadiza's daughter, carried a ask of oil to anoint the prophet's head as was also customary for an honored guest. They instinctively knew what their mistress would require.

Elisha was impressed at the reception he was given by this rather extraordinary lady. He has visited houses of many rich and noble people, but this reception was a step above any of those. It was special—it was from the heart. She was sincerely interested in his well-being contrary to most who received him. Most received him out of fear, but she seemed to be driven to care for him. He looked for the husband as it was customary for the husband to greet any guest, no matter what their station—rich or poor, noble, or common, it was a husband's duty to greet all guests that were dining in the house—but Saana was nowhere to be found. The prophet didn't know that the husband wasn't informed until after he was in the house; everything had happened so fast. When Saana was informed of Marta's guest, true to form, he impolitely stayed in the fields. His wife's guests were of no interest to him, especially going out of his way to entertain them when he had work to do. His ignorance of social courtesies or blatant rudeness was of no consequence to him.

Marta directed her servants to offer only the best of their food and wine. She was not sure why, but she was compelled to honor this man in every way possible. She somehow knew that he was not an ordinary person, although why he was so special eluded her—for now.

She talked to Gehazi at length about his adventures and had Gehazi interpret any questions she had for Elisha. She was trying to be careful not to ask too many questions, yet she was very curious about this mysterious man. There was something profoundly powerful about his presence, and she just had to know more. She asked Gehazi, "I heard about you leaving with this man and how quickly it happened. Was it hard to leave Shunem? I don't think I could ever leave." She stopped for a moment and then said, "I'm sorry, but I just thought about it. I don't know the man's name."

Gehazi suddenly felt a little embarrassed; all this happened so fast he barely had time to think let alone give introductions. "His name is Elisha, and he is a prophet of the Hebrew God, Yahweh. He is feared even in kings' courts. Wherever he goes, people move out of his way. He has several followers who are disciples that learn from him at his house on Mt. Carmel. I have not met a man like him. Even my father fears him."

"Your father?" Marta said with surprise. "I have never seen your father afraid of anyone."

Gehazi looked down, nodded his head, smiled, and said, "He fears this man, and with good reason. This man moves the heart of kings and religious leaders alike. He is a good man though, who has a generous heart and has helped many people. I have grown to respect him very much."

"How often will you be coming to Shunem?" she asked.

Gehazi looked up in thought and said, "Lately every month for the first new moon. Many people are coming every month to see the Hebrew prophet. He is a legend in most of the world, and now he will be in Shunem."

Marta went silent and watched Elisha as he ate. He seemed to be in perpetual thought. Never had she meet anyone so mystifying. Even with her keen knack for sizing people up, this man was perplexing to her. She found him kind, well-mannered, and quiet—one who kept his responses to her questions short and to the point. It was obvious to her that he was not trying to hide anything; he just didn't feel the need to elaborate.

Elisha leaned over and said something to Gehazi, and they looked at her in a way that made her feel very self-conscious. "Is there a problem?" she asked.

"No, no problem," Gehazi responded. "He just commented about your eyes and how striking they were. We rarely see gray eyes among the Hebrews. I hope it did not offend you."

A little red-faced from embarrassment, she said, "No, he didn't offend me. I hope that having gray eyes is not a bad thing. It's something I can't fix—not like I can if we served sour wine or something else embarrassing."

Gehazi smiled. "On the contrary, he thinks they are beautiful as well as unique. He was also wondering where your husband was and if he somehow offended your husband."

Uncomfortable, Marta's face turned a little red again. "He is out working the fields with the servants. He is an extremely hard worker and had a lot of work to do today."

Gehazi interpreted, and the prophet made a reply, again Gehazi translated to Marta. "My master understands. Farm work is extremely hard and never seems to end. He had hoped to meet your husband before we had to leave, but it won't be today. We must leave now. There is work to do before tonight's festivities on the hilltop above the marketplace. We thank you for the food and rest from the heat."

With that, Elisha said something to Gehazi, and they both stood up. Marta stood up and bowed to the prophet and said, "Please feel free to stop here anytime you pass by. There will always be food and wine whenever you do."

With that, both men said their goodbyes and left heading toward Shunem.

Marta felt a tinge of regret when they left. She still had so many questions she wanted to ask. Was he always a prophet? What part of Israel did he come from? Did he have a family? And so on. She thought to herself, *Oh well, if they will be here for every first new moon, I would have lots of opportunity to ask more questions and get to know this mysterious man. This prophet of the Hebrew God.*

*****

The next month's first new moon came, and as sure as the rising of the sun, Elisha and Gehazi appeared. She had the boy Lamel, now a young man, keep an eye out for them. "They are coming! I can see them, mistress, I can see them!" He was excited at the opportunity to do something he felt was important. At twenty, he was nearly a grown man but still had a lot of little boy in him. Marta and Lo met Gehazi and the prophet as they approached the house.

"Come in and rest and eat something. We have a new wine that Gehazi's father brought us, it's excellent," Marta said with delight. She pointed to Lo and said, "This is Lo, a man of great wisdom and education. He was a teacher in Egypt and now teaches me." Lo looked down with embarrassment. He thought to himself, *Will she ever learn proper decorum? I am a servant not a family member or a social equal. Will she ever learn?* He looked at both men and said, "I am an Egyptian and her servant as well as her teacher, and I am at your service."

Elisha, smiling, said something to Gehazi while looking at Lo. Gehazi interpreted, "You are more than a servant of this fine lady. My master can see you're a friend and more than a friend but something akin to family. He can also see you are a man of fine character, and my master said he will be looking forward to hearing more about your life in Egypt." The statement took Lo and Marta by surprise. This prophet was not only perceptive but gracious to anyone no matter their station in life. Marta took a mental note and decided she would be more careful in her conversations with this man who can hear the heart as well as hear a person's words.

After Gehazi and the prophet left, Marta made up her mind that the only way she could learn more about this man and get to know him better was to have the prophet stay at her house while they were in town. She went to her husband who was having his own supper in the courtyard and asked him to build an additional room for the prophet on the roof of the house with an outside entrance so she could keep busy-body tongues from elicit gossip. Not that she cared much about gossip, but her family might get offended at the gossip, and they would care a great deal, especially her father the businessman. She saw that he had just finished his meal and was standing up when she spoke, "Husband, may I have a word with you?"

Saana looked at her with a blank face and said, "What do you want now?"

She replied, "The man who Gehazi travels with and has stopped here for a few meals, well, I perceive he is a man of God, and I would like to honor him with a room that he could turn into whenever they pass this way. Can I have a room built for him on the roof where the air is cooler in the evening? Gehazi tells me that he stays with his family while he and the prophet are in town, and the prophet stays at an inn—"

Saana abruptly interrupted her. "Yes, yes. Build your room for this 'man of God' or whatever you call him, do whatever you want. Just leave me out of it. I'm too busy to be bothered with the details."

Marta had Gamal built a room next to the wall on the roof where there was better access to the evening breeze. It was a large room with a bed for the prophet, a cabinet for storage, and a table and two chairs. There were two large windows with lattice over them for privacy. She also ensured there was a lamp on the table that would always be full when he came to the room.

The next new moon, she had Lamel on watch again; and he, faithful as always, shouted, "They are coming, mistress, they are almost here." Marta and Lamel ran out to meet them before they passed by. As was her custom now, she invited them to come in, and after they had eaten, she said, "I have a surprise for you. If you both could follow me, I will show you my surprise." She escorted them to the roof, climbing the stairs from the streetside of the house and proudly showed them the room. There were pillows on Elisha's bed as well as several blankets. The two chairs were large and sturdy and ornately decorated, and the table was large enough for both men to eat at comfortably. It was not a thrown-together shack but a comfortable room that was well built with both the building and furnishings showing there was considerable thought invested in its construction.

Elisha said through Gehazi, "This is a complete surprise. I never expected anything quite like this. This is an outstanding room." Gehazi explained to Marta what the prophet said. Then wearing a huge smile, Marta excused herself and left.

Elisha went over and laid on the bed and found it soft and comfortable. He looked around the room again and admired the craftsmanship in both the furnishings and the room itself. Marta obviously spared no expense and had thought out every detail. He looked over at Gehazi and said, "We must do something for this lady after all the work and expense she has shown us. Call her and have her come. I want to speak to her." Gehazi went to her in the kitchen and told her that his master wanted to talk to her. She followed Gehazi to the new room; and she, without hesitation, walked right into the room and up to the side of Elisha's bed where he was laying. Her boldness in entering the room was startling enough, but her walking right up to the bed a man was laying in, up to a man that was not her husband, was beyond bold; it was scandalous. Elisha was unfazed. He looked her in the eyes and did an assessment of this courageous and bold woman. Oh, she was beautiful for sure, but the thing that struck him more than anything else about her was her indomitable spirit. He believed that no matter what the obstacle she would never quit or give up. She was a queen in a world of ordinary people.

Without taking his eyes from hers, he said, "Gehazi, tell her I want to repay her for all the kindness she has shown us. Let her know I could ask the king for a favor on her behalf, or I could talk to the commander of the army for her. Whatever she wants, if it is within my power, I will give it."

Gehazi was perplexed. He had never seen his master offer such a thing, and he hesitated. "Go ahead and tell her what I offered," Elisha said, growing impatient. Gehazi managed to stammer out, "My… my master has just offered to go to the king or the commander of the army on your behalf. I have never seen him do such a thing since I have been with him. He must find you incredibly special indeed."

The look on Marta's face was like one who had just been deeply insulted. "I don't need anything from him. I live among my own people and live my life as I see fit. I don't need anything from your master." And with that, she turned and left the room in an abrupt and angry manner.

Elisha looked at Gehazi with a surprised look on his face. "I certainly didn't expect that reaction. You would have thought that I had insulted her in a most horrible way. There must be something I can do for her. You know these people. Can you think of anything?"

Gehazi responded, "I used to know her when she was a child. I have not been around the family for a long time. What I do know, though, is that she has no children, and her husband is an old man."

Elisha stared at the ground for a minute, looked up excitedly, and said, "Call her back in. I have more to say to her."

 Gehazi went and found her in the courtyard and asked, "Would you please come back to the room? My master has more to tell you."

Gehazi could tell she was still upset and thought it was about what the prophet had offered, but that was not the issue at all. No, not even close. She had a request she would have loved to ask, but she was terrified to utter it. She had one wish above all others and dreaded even the hope that it would come true. She wanted this man of God to tell her she was going to have a child, a son. Of all things in life, she would give everything to have a son. But the thought of hoping one more time and having those hopes dashed was more than she could stand and when Elisha didn't mention it a silent frustration exploded in her.

She followed Gehazi back to the room, but she could not get her feet to move when she tried to step inside. She couldn't bring herself to cross the threshold. She was more terrified now than she had ever been in her life. She tried to talk, but the words would not come. She just froze at the door. She was trembling; beads of sweat formed on her forehead and she thought she was going to faint just as she had when her father announced her betrothal. Gehazi saw it and was confused by her reaction. This man could give her just about anything she asked for, and here she was acting like a young child about to be punished.

Elisha looked her straight in the eyes and with a smile and a firm loud voice made the pronouncement, "This time next year, you will hold a son." Gehazi interpreted and smiled. The words hit Marta so hard it took her breath away. It was like someone had punched her in the stomach. Her head was swimming, and she was trying to breathe but couldn't. She tried to speak, but nothing would come out. She grabbed the sides of the doorway to keep from falling. Finally, she was able to take a breath and managed to shout out, "Don't lie to me, man of God! Just, just don't lie to me." Both Elisha and Gehazi were stunned.

Marta turned immediately and ran down the stairs, through the house and into her room. Tears were streaming down her cheeks. She ran over to her bed and began to throw her pillows and blankets and turn over furniture. She screamed at the top of her lungs. The shock and the pain were unbearable. She threw herself on her bed, shouting, "How could he! How could he torture me like that!" Just when she had finally let go of all hope and resigned herself to a childless future, this man had the audacity to tell her to hope again. She shouted, "I am not going to hope for a child! I am not! If he is a man of God, does he not have enough discernment to know the pain he just caused me?"

Hadiza came running to the room when she heard all the commotion. "What is wrong, mistress? Are you all right? This room is a mess. Did the master attack you again? Speak to me so I can help you."

Marta looked at her from the bed and sobbed. "Why did he do that? I had given up on having a child, and he started the torment all over again. Why? Why?" She stopped crying, sat at the end of the bed, and just stared at the oor, whispering over and over, "Why?"

Hadiza was confused. Who was she talking about? Was she talking about Saana? What did that monster do to her now? "Are you talking about Saana? What did he do now?" Marta responded with an exasperated tone.

"Not Saana. I would have expected that, and it would have been much easier to brush that off. No, I am talking about the prophet. He hurt me more than anyone has ever hurt me."

Hadiza blurted out, "How? What did he do? I will personally take a club to him! How dare he hurt you after all you have done for him. After all the kindness you showed him. How could he be so heartless? I think I will go and find a staff and strike him on the side of his head as hard as I can!" Her blood was boiling.

Just as she turned to leave, Marta said, "No, it is nothing like that. I think he was trying to show me a kindness, but he just didn't know my history or my situation with Saana. He told me I was going to hold a child, a son, by this time next year. Something I so wanted to hear—until I did. I'm scared, I'm so scared." Marta started to tear up again. "If he only knew how hurtful that was, how impossible it is. Just leave him alone. He just didn't know. He was trying to be kind but just didn't know."

Hadiza took in a deep breath and walked over and sat down next to Marta. She put her arm around her, and they both started to cry.

7

Agreed

It was midsummer, and the last time Elisha stopped by Marta's house was early spring; he hadn't been in Shunem since. It was unusual that the prophet would not come to Shunem for so many weeks. Marta began to think that she had somehow offended the man. Her reaction the last time she saw him was not good when he was only trying to be kind to her. She refused even to eat with him and didn't talk to him before he left. Her fear of disappointment at that time caused her to avoid him at all costs. She was afraid he would prophesy about the baby again and that terri ed her. From a window that day, she watched Elisha leave, she saw him take a turn in the road and look toward her house for several minutes. She was sure there was no way he could see her, but something in the way he stared back toward her house made her believe otherwise. It left her with the oddest feeling—it was like he was saying, "Trust me." She just could not bring herself to believe or trust anyone about having a baby. It wasn't until the prophet's declaration that she realized how badly it was affecting her. It had been wearing her down, and she hadn't recognized how bad—that is, until now.

It was one month later, and Marta had pretty much put the whole prophet episode out of her mind. She was busy making sure the temporary workers Saana had hired to work the harvest were fed and was busy putting out little fires with the household staff. Saana was grumpier than he usually was for this time of year, but she had learned to manage that with food and avoidance. Feed him good food and stay out of his way. But as Saana grew older, he got crankier and harder to console or to avoid.

This particular day, however, he was being especially difficult. When the day ended, Saana would usually sit in the courtyard and eat his meal by himself. But this evening, he never even touched his meal and was drinking heavily. By the time the moon was up, he was inebriated and foul and had worked himself into a rage. All the household went to their rooms early to avoid his abusive behavior, and Marta did the same.

Marta was just getting into bed when Saana showed up at her door and kicked it open. Before she could protest, he shouted and yelled profanities at her and started shoving her around. He struck her on the face and shoulders several times and threw her on the bed. He was at his ugliest. As she started to break down, she decided not to fight and let him do his worst. After all years and all her shattered plans, she began to surrender and resign herself to all hope of fulfilled ambitions. She conceded in her thoughts, *What's the use in all that planning?*

Hadiza heard the crashing of the door and furniture being thrown around and Saana yelling at the top of his lungs; so after waiting a few minutes, she worked up the courage, although terrified, and hurried to her mistress's room. When she entered the room, she saw Marta lying there, battered and bruised, with a vacant stare. It was the look on Marta's face that bothered Seima the most. She had never seen Marta look as if she were a dead person and never would have believed it was even possible, but there she was. Hadiza quietly walked over to Marta, took a pitcher of water, and soaked a towel that was on the table next to the bed. Sitting next to Marta, she gently put her arm around her and started to wipe away the dirt and blood, trying to sooth the bruises. Hadiza muttered to herself, "How I hate that man. Justice will prevail, I truly believe justice will prevail!"

Marta looked empty, beaten, not just physically but spiritually as well. The look worried Hadiza a great deal. She had seen that look on other people but never on Marta. In her experience, whenever she saw that look on people, it almost always had a dreadful ending.

Hadiza called out for Michael to bring a cup of wine for her mistress. "Mistress, please drink some of this wine, it will help," Hadiza pleaded as she pressed a cup to Marta's lips. Marta drank a sip, then a gulp, and then she grabbed it with both hands and drained the cup. Marta looked at her friend and said, "If only the prophet hadn't promised the one thing that can never happen, I could continue to ght, continue to stand up to the monster, but I have lost any hope that my life will ever be anything but miserable. I have you and the others, but I have no real life. My dreams are lost in an unful lled promise. Oh, Hadiza, I hurt, I hurt so miserably. My heart hurts, my body hurts, my very soul hurts. I am defeated." She began to sob uncontrollably. Hadiza didn't say anything; she just held her friend closer. Her heart smoldered with anger toward Saana, toward the unfairness of it all, and finally toward the God of Elisha.

The morning sun broke through Marta's lattice and lled the room with a warm light. She had fallen asleep with Hadiza tenderly holding her mistress the whole time. Hadiza slowly lowered Marta back and covered her with a blanket and silently left the room. She instructed Michael to stand by the room and to not disturb her mistress but to let her sleep until she woke up on her own.

Several hours later, Marta awoke aching and sore all over because of the bruises on her body. She rubbed at the caked blood on her chin and nose, and tried to stretch out her stiffness, when suddenly she saw a man dressed in a white tunic sitting on the end of her bed, just smiling. Shocked and startled, her heart began to pound as she clutched her bedding. Although she was terrified, there seemed to be a comforting eminence about him that assured her that he was no threat. She could somehow sense and even smell a warm, sweet aroma that was soothing and strangely healing.

She sat up in the bed and asked with an uneasy voice, "Who… who are you?"

The only answer she heard was a quiet voice saying, "Everything is going to be all right. Don't despair, everything is going to be all right." His words were reassuring like a warm, healing balm. Instead of being fearful of a strange man sitting on her bed, unexpectedly, she felt consoled and safe. "Who are you?" she asked again, this time not with an apprehensive voice but as if she were thanking someone that had just done her a great favor. The man reached out, laid his hand on her head, and repeated again, "Everything is going to be all right. Just trust in the God of Elisha and you will see."

Suddenly, he was gone. He just vanished into thin air. She thought, "I must be dreaming." She looked around the room then got out of bed and sat in a chair, and while sitting there, she just stared out the window. *It couldn't be a dream,* she thought. The moment that thought came to her, she realized her heart had been healed—the hole in her soul was mended; she felt she was alive again! She just didn't feel alive physically, but the embers of hope once again burned within her. She was alive all over! Marta sat there for a few minutes gazing at the place where the man had sat trying to absorb what had just happened. Then deep inside she discerned that she had just been visited by an angel of God—not any of the Shunem gods—but an angel of the God of Elisha. A peaceful feeling embraced her, and a newfound strength bubbled up from within. A smile replaced her stinging tears and fresh determination emerged in her very soul; she was back—the true Marta was back!

Marta called out to Michael who was still sitting outside her door. "Bring me lots of water," Marta ordered. "I intend to bathe straight away. Also, bring me some food and a little wine. I will eat something while you get the bath water ready."

Michael was confused and slow to respond. From what Hadiza had described, she had expected to see a woman who had been beaten, was terribly sad, and in a lot of pain, both physically and emotionally; but here was their mistress standing tall and in full command like nothing had happened. She could see the cuts, the blood, and the bruises and could tell that her mistress was obviously in some pain, but despite it all, she was standing there her old self again. "Did you hear me? I said bring me some food. Quit staring and get to it, silly girl," Marta said with some humor in her voice.

"Yes, mistress. Right away. Water, food, wine, right away, yes, right away." And Michael ran down the hallway full of excitement.

Michael hurried into the kitchen and ran up to Hadiza and shouted, "She is all right! She is all right! She wants water for bathing, but first she wants food and some wine. She called me into her room and gave me the orders right then. She caught me off guard after you told me what the master did to her. She looks a mess and is in some pain, but she's all right." Michael then frantically went about the kitchen getting some bread and meat for her mistress. "Don't forget the wine. I mustn't forget the wine," she said, bursting with joy.

Hadiza followed Michael back to Marta's room, and they found her sitting on one of the chairs talking to a sparrow in the window no more than a foot away from Marta's face. Marta was smiling as she talked to the bird. At first, this concerned Hadiza. She thought that maybe Marta had snapped and was delusional but was quickly put at ease when Marta turned to her and said, "Hadiza, I am so glad to see you! Sank you for sitting with me last night. I was beyond a doubt at the lowest point in my life. I needed a friend, and you were that friend. Last night, I had never felt so distraught and without hope, so beaten. But this morning, an angel of the God of Elisha came to me and spoke to me. He said, 'Everything is going to be all right,' and then he laid his hands on my head and again said 'Everything is going to be all right,' then he just vanished. One instant he was there, and the next instant he was gone. He just disappeared.

"When he talked, I felt he was saying to me, 'Trust in the God of Elisha, and it will all be good. It will all be good.' Suddenly, I felt my strength return to me. I felt my spirit healed of its despair. I felt whole again. I felt alive again. I can feel myself rising out of the ashes. I know it sounds strange, but I feel renewed, like a new person." Somehow and despite all appearances it all made sense to Hadiza. She somehow knew her friend had just been visited by an angel. Marta's countenance and her vigor let Hadiza know that a miracle had just happened. Last night, Marta was at the end of her rope, and this morning, she was full of life again; she was the old Marta they had not seen in months.

Marta ate and bathed then proceeded to go about the house, directing the staff as if she were sixteen again. She was singing, joking, teasing and laughing again, and full of happiness the staff teased her back. The atmosphere of the whole house changed that day.

That night, a very tired Saana crawled into bed and was sleeping soundly after a hard day in the elds and never heard the footsteps of a lady full of cold intent enter the room. Marta quietly walked up to the side of the bed and pulled the covers up over Saana's arms, then she slowly got on the bed and stood on her feet and jumped down to her knees, pinning Saana's arms under the blankets. Saana woke up with a shock to nd a knife pointed at his throat. He heard her say, "I promised you what would happen if you ever hurt me again, did you not believe me? Now I have a promise to ful ll, I have my word to keep, and I will keep it with great joy." She started to press on the handle of the knife, and Saana's eyes were wild with fear as the point pressed against the skin, and he suddenly screamed.

Marta stopped, smiled, and said, "But there is one other option." She leaned close to his face, "You will never stay in this house again. You will never step foot in this house again. If I need anything, I will nd you. Is that clear?" She pressed the knife against his throat just a little harder until the tip was just breaking the skin. "Well?"

Saana looked at her in terror. Panic had locked his vocal cords; he couldn't speak so he just nodded his head. Marta leaned back and said, "Good, then we are agreed." She climbed off the bed and stood at the side of the bed and asked, "Have you nothing more to say to me? Is there anything you feel you need to say?" He stood up in the bed, and his look of terror now turned to a look of rage, and he screamed out, "I will kill you for this. You should have killed me when you had the chance, now I will do what you could not."

With that, he jumped off the bed and started to walk toward her. She stood her ground and said, "Kill me tonight, and by the time the sun goes down tomorrow, you will be dead yourself. You will have used up all your chances. As a matter of fact, you better pray none of my family come to visit me in the next several days, you bruised me up badly. In that case, you will already be a dead man. You have done your worst, and still, you do not scare me. So if you intend to kill me now, do it. Otherwise, we have an agreement and I expect you to stick to it."

With that, Saana stopped. He knew she was right. He knew that if any of her relatives saw her with the bruises she had, either the prince or her father would hear about it and, without a doubt, kill him. He knew that his actions last night could very well be his death sentence. His only hope was to follow through on their agreement; forced or not, he didn't have a choice. There was no other alternative. There was no other way out of his predicament. He stopped and, with his sts clenched, looked down and nodded. Marta smiled and said, "Good, then there will never be a repeat of last night. Sat would not be good for either one of us." Then she turned and walked to her room.

That morning, she instructed Lo to assist in moving Saana's things to one of the barns. The look on Lo's face was at first of delight, then one of open fear. He asked with trepidation in his voice, "He has agreed to this?"

Marta laughed and said, "Yes, as a matter of fact, he has. Just ask him where he wants his belongings and follow his directions. Do it respectfully but do it." Lo nodded his head, still with a look of shock on his face. It was a look Marta thought she would remember the rest of her life.

8
Excitement and Humiliation

The next few weeks were quiet with Saana staying away from the house entirely. There was considerably more laughing and smiling throughout the house. There was a lightness and sense of happiness that the servants had not seen in the house for years. Saana had constructed a makeshift bedroom in the largest barn and was served his food by Lo. The staff treated him respectfully as Marta had ordered but were still wary of him. Whenever they laughed very loud, they would all stop and look for Saana to come bursting in; it never happened. Slowly, the servants were becoming accustomed to their newfound freedom. To them, though, he was a poisonous snake that could never be trusted, so they were always a little on guard, keeping one guarding eye on the door while going about their day.

Marta was going about redecorating the house inside and out. She had spent a great deal of money, but Saana never said a word of complaint. The house was looking like a mansion now.

One morning, as she was getting ready for breakfast, a wave of nausea came over her. She put it off as just being tired, but strangely the smell of food suddenly made her sick to her stomach and feeling more nauseous by the minute. She stood up to let Hadiza know how she was feeling and nearly passed out, saying to herself, "I'm never sick." She slowly went into the kitchen and saw Hadiza kneading the bread and started to say how she was feeling when the room started spinning. The next thing Marta was aware of was looking up into Lo's face, hearing him say, "Well, hello again. I remember a similar situation from a long time ago. Are you all right?"

She sat up and was a bit embarrassed. "I don't know what happened. I started to feel sick and was going to say something to Hadiza, and suddenly, I am looking up at you. I think I need to go back to my room and lie down." Hadiza was kneeling next to Lo and said, "I will help you get there. Come, Lo, help her to her feet, and I will assist her to her room."

Once she and Hadiza got to her room, she closed the door and assisted Marta to a chair. "How long have you been feeling ill?"

Marta said with a quiver in her voice, "Three or four days, but nothing like today. Why? Do you know what's wrong with me? I'm never sick. Not even as a child did I ever get sick. What could possibly be wrong?"

"What about your monthly cycle? Have you noticed any changes?" Hadiza asked, studying her mistress's face.

"I don't know. I haven't had one this month. Is that why I'm sick? What sickness causes that to happen?" Marta asked with an almost panicked tone in her voice.

Hadiza smiled and tears started to well up in her eyes.

Marta blurted out, "Is it bad? I can see your tears. It's bad, isn't it?"

Hadiza started laughing, and that startled Marta. "No, my dear, dear friend. No, not at all. Unless you consider having a baby a bad thing." Hadiza leaned back and laughed. "Silly girl, you are pregnant. You are going to have a baby. Your dreams are coming true."

Marta stared at Hadiza in disbelief; the thought of pregnancy never even came into her mind. Since that long night a few weeks ago, she had not even thought about having a baby. She was somewhere between shock and denial, along with the refusal to even let that come to mind. Marta said with a voice sounding choked, "What do you mean I'm going to have a baby? You know how hurtful it is to me to joke about that. Don't tease me! Please don't tease me!" And tears started to well up in her eyes, "I just couldn't take it. Please don't tease me."

Hadiza reached over and gently touched her hand and said, "Mistress, I would never tease you about this. I have sat up with you too many nights not to understand what this means to you. You are going to have a baby. You are with child. My heart sings for you right now. There will be such a celebration as never has been seen in Shunem. When you are feeling better, let's go to your mother and tell her. Let's let the world know. Let's let that…that old snake of a man know that what he meant for evil has turned to good. Sat ought to torment him like nothing else could."

Marta was trying to soak it all in. She was still having a hard time getting past her own unbelief. After all this time, after all her tears, after all her prayers, was she really going to have a baby? Excitement slowly started to rise in her. She fought against the refusal to believe it. Her mind was spinning. So many thoughts were running through her mind. First thoughts of excitement then thoughts of the so many what-ifs. "What if Hadiza is wrong, and this is just a false alarm? What if something happens while I'm pregnant and I lose the baby?" What if…what if? The "what if's" wouldn't stop. Marta grabbed Hadiza's hand and said, "Are you sure? Are you sure? Is there any way you can be mistaken? A baby? I'm going to have a baby! Are you sure?"

Hadiza smiled and gently closed her hand around Marta's and looked her directly in the eyes and said, "I have never been surer of anything in my life. In trying to hurt you, that old snake has given you your dream. I can't wait to see the look on his face when he nds out. That will be something, yes, that will really be something. Yes, my dear you are de nitely going to have baby. Congratulations! Now let's go tell that old snake."

Marta smiled and thought to herself, *Maybe it's really true. After all that Saana has put me through and out of his spite and rage, he has inadvertently given me my one dream.* With a sarcastic smile and a mock irritated tone, she looked at Hadiza and said, "Watch what you call him now. After all, he is the father of my baby." Both started laughing until the tears of laughter were owing down their cheeks.

Saana was in the smallest of the barns tending to a young calf when the ladies came in. He saw them and immediately was angry. "What are you doing in here? If I can't have access to my own house, I can at least have some peace in my own barns. What do you want?"

Hadiza answered first, "We have some news for you. Some very exciting news. But I will let the mistress tell you."

Marta walked up to an arm's length from Saana and smiled and said, "I'm going to have a baby. Did you hear? I am with child. You gave me my dream. That's all I wanted to say, and now we will leave you to your work. We just thought it was right to tell you first before we told anybody else. Now I am going to my family's house for a short while to tell them, but we just wanted to say congratulations… Papa." Marta could hardly keep from laughing and dancing, but she felt that would push Saana beyond his ability to restrain himself. She might not be afraid for herself, but now she had a baby to think about. How Saana would react was one of the "what-ifs."

Saana was dumbstruck. The very thing he didn't want; the one thing he knew tortured Marta more than anything was never having a child. Out of his blind anger and hatred for her and in his drunken stupidity, he had given up that one thing he had over her. He wanted to lash out now more than ever before, but he also wanted to live. He started to stammer and tried to saysomething, but there were no words. He turned and stomped out of the barn and started barking and snapping at one of the eld hands to vent his anger.

Marta and Hadiza went back to the house, and Marta told Hadiza she could inform the other servants of the good news but no one outside of the staff. Then she called Michael and told her the news herself and instructed her to go with her to her family's house while she broke the news to them. Michael was ecstatic and let out an ear-piercing squeal that made Marta squint.

"A baby! You're going to have a baby?" She let out another squeal. Marta winced and said, "Yes, I'm going to have a baby. Now would you stop that infernal noise? My parents could probably hear you right now it's so loud, and I'd rather tell them myself if you don't mind."

It was a twenty-minute walk to her parents' house, and it seemed like hours. Michael saw one of her parents' neighbors and almost said something when Marta said, with a loud and commanding voice, "Michael!" stopping Michael in her tracks. On the other hand, Marta herself was so excited she wanted to run up and down the street yelling, "I'm going to have a baby!" but she wanted her family to know before the rest of the town. She felt sixteen all over again.

She turned to Michael. "Hush, girl. Have you not heard word I said? I want to let my parents know. Now get behind me and follow me the rest of the way, and for goodness' sake, keep quiet when we get to my parents' house!"

When they arrived at the house, Si, the female servant who was Marta's age, came to the door and ran over and gave her a hug. "It's so good to see you. It has been a while since your last visit. You look wonderful. I will run and let your mother know you are here." With her excitement, she forgot her manners, and she wheeled around and ran into the house, leaving Marta and Michael standing on the porch. Marta smiled and opened the door and walked into the main room. Just then, her mother came from the kitchen into the room, still brushing something off the front of her dress. Sonta ran over to Marta and hugged her and gave her a kiss on the cheek.

"Where have you been? It's been almost two months since you last came by the house. You look wonderful. Come, please, both of you, sit down and rest your feet. Are you well? How about that rascal of a husband of yours?"

Marta said, "We are all well, but there is some news I would like to share, some very happy news." She sat there quietly smiling in a way that she knew would torment her mother, and when she could tell her mother was about toburst, she laughed and yelled out, "I'm going to have a baby! I am with child. God has smiled on me, and I'm going to have a baby."

Sonta stopped dgeting over Marta and just stared for a minute. Her mouth fell open, but nothing came out. Then tears started to well up in her eyes. She looked down and grabbed Marta's hand and then pulled her over and gave her daughter a huge hug. She started to cry out with delight. The squeal was loud enough that several of the servants came to see if there was a problem. Sonta jumped up and started to shout out all kinds of plans: "We must celebrate. We must have a feast and celebrate! We must invite all our friends and celebrate! Oh, this is a happy day! We must let everyone know right away! Marta is going to have a baby! Oh, what a happy day!" Marta and Michael were laughing at her mother's exuberance. Marta had never seen her mother act this way. She was like a child getting the best present she had ever been given. Her mother was hugging and squeezing Marta, Michael, and all her servants as well. The sight made Marta even more happy—as if that were possible.

Sonta stopped hugging people and turned becoming suddenly serious, "What does Saana think? What did he say when you told him? I remember when you finally told me that he was using the idea of no baby to torture you. That man is an absolute monster."

Marta, also with a serious look on her face, said, "He said nothing, not a thing. I believe he was angry that he lost his one hold over my head. It was the only way he could torment me. But here I am with child, and he can do nothing about it. I am the happiest I have ever been in my life. Happier than when I turned sixteen, and you know how happy I was that day. Now I have a future that's more than just living or living just to torment Saana." Then she said with a sneering smile, "Though that was fun in itself."

"Where is Father?" Marta asked, looking around. Her mother stopped jumping around for a minute, smiled, and said, "He is on his way back from a business trip to Megiddo. He should be back later today. He will be delighted with the news. He has changed so much since you married Saana. He so regrets betrothing you to him. He told me he was so busy trying to save the business that he never realized how much you meant to him until he married you off to that horrible excuse of a man. Oh my, how he will celebrate when he hears the news. Come, let's tell the neighbors."

They spent the next two hours talking and celebrating, and then Marta regretfully uttered, "I have to be going back to my house. It will be dark soon, and I don't like to be out in the street after dark." Her mother embraced her once more then saw them off.

When Marta arrived back home, there was some commotion at the front of the house. Saana was drunk, yelling at Lo and demanding to go in the house. And Lo stated he was under the mistress's orders not to let him in. Saana picked up a stick and was about to hit Lo when Marta yelled out, "What's the problem here? What are you doing with that stick? Didn't we have an agreement? I expect you to abide by it."

Saana whirled around and went to strike Marta with it when Lo grabbed his arm and pulled the stick from Saana's hand. Saana was stronger than Lo, but he also was very drunk. Saana yelled at Lo, "I will have you hanged for that! Do you hear me? Hanged!"

Marta calmly stepped forward and got inches from Saana's face and said, "You will have no one hanged. You will go back to your room and sleep off this poor excuse for behavior and leave the staff and the house alone."

Saana exploded back, "You are a whore! You are with child, and I don't believe it's mine. Do you hear me? I don't believe it's mine."

Marta smiled. "I have too many witnesses that can vouch for my whereabouts since you attacked me that night. The servants will corroborate the viciousness of that attack. I think I am just going to invite my family over for dinner and have my servants explain just how I got pregnant. What do you think, Lo? Do you think that would be a good idea? My family loves you and all the adventures you tell them about. Do you think they would believe you or your master? Never mind. I don't want to put you in that position right now. We will just wait until my family gets here. What do you think, husband? How well do you think my family will take this accusation of yours?" Marta then reached over to the table she was standing near and broke off a piece of bread from a loaf that was on a platter, took a bite, and smiled as she chewed, keeping her stare locked on Saana until he lowered his gaze. Saana mumbled to himself and left the house, slamming the door behind him.

Marta turned to the servants and, with a commanding voice, said, "Bar the doors tonight. I don't trust him. I think he will try to get even with me tonight. He had only one thing he could hold over my head, and now that's gone. He hates Lo and Hadiza. I think he would love to hurt anyone of us tonight. We need to keep watch. I will stay up until midnight. Lamel, you take the next two hours. Lo, the next two, and, Gamal, you take the watch untilsunrise. Be vigilant, Saana is mean and cruel beyond words, and if you let your guard down, he will have no mercy. I believe he will try and make it look like a robber broke in and that way try to avoid blame, and in the process, he will make as many of you pay as well." All of them knew just how serious the situation was, but they also knew it would be short-lived. Saana never stayed focused on anything for very long other than business; he lived and breathed his business. If he tries something tonight and is caught, it is doubtful he will try anything again. He really fears Marta's family and the idea that if he tried something and got caught, it would surely mean Marta's family would be paying him a visit.

It was late into Gamal's watch, and as he was fighting off sleep, he heard someone trying to crawl through a space in the kitchen replace where the cooking fire was next to the wall. Gamal was instantly wide awake and reached over and tapped Lo on the shoulder. Lo had laid down in a space in the kitchen just in case Gamal needed any assistance. Lo quietly got to his feet and grabbed a large stirring stick. Gamal picked up a piece of firewood, and they both walked over to where the person was trying to get in. As soon as one of the person's arms came into view, they both hit it as hard as they could. There was a scream, and they could hear the person run off, moaning. Gamal and Lo were both shaken, and both stayed on guard until the sun came up.

Later that morning, they reported everything to Marta and let her know what had happened and asked if they should continue to stand guard that evening as well. She thought for a minute and said, "No, I think he got the message. Besides, I think you hurt him pretty badly, and if you did, he won't be coming back anytime soon. But I would like Lo to go to my parents' house and invite them to eat with us tonight. I believe that will put a special kind of fear in Saana." She knew that the sight of her family at the house would terrify him. She thought to herself, *I may or may not tell them of the accusation, but he won't know that and will not sleep well for some time to come.*

Lo went to Marta's parents' house, and when he returned, he let Marta know that he had invited the whole family, and they all accepted, including her brothers with their families.

"It will be a regular feast," he boasted. "Your father had just arrived back home, and he is very excited about the news about the baby, and he can't wait to see you."

Hadiza was not as pleased and complained, "Today! This evening? Do you know what position you have put me in? How will get everything ready by then?"

Marta turned to Hadiza and said, "Relax. It is my family, not the king and his family. We will all help get things ready. Remember why we are doing this. I believe this will put an extra level of fear in Saana and help ensure a lasting peace in the house. So let's get to it."

Then Marta started to bring out a basket of grain to grind, then she looked at the others in the room just watching and said, "Come, come, let's get to it." Gamal went to get rewood for cooking, and the rest started busying themselves with the different tasks in getting ready for a small feast. Before long, there was a smell of meat cooking and bread baking. Hadiza was still fretting, but that was nothing new, she always had a tough time not being in control in any demanding situation. She was a great and loyal friend but a bit of a worrier as well.

Lo took a wagon to Gehazi's father's house to get more wine and to ask Gehazi's father for any news of the prophet or his son. Elisha and his assistant had not been to Shunem in months, and he was wondering if there had been any news concerning them. There was none. Gehazi's father had not heard from or seen Gehazi since he and Elisha's last visit several months ago. Having bought the wine Lo started back home and was trying to figure out why there had been no sign of or word from the prophet in such a long time. He usually came to town once or twice a month. He thought to himself with a smile, *He is probably in some king's palace busy terrifying everybody.* Lo remembered when he heard about how Marta had reacted to Elisha's prophetic word about her having a baby. It wasn't until then that he realized how much not having a child affected her. Well now that she is with child, he would love to see the prophet's reaction to the news or Marta's reaction at seeing the prophet again.

Marta sent Michael to watch from the street corner to let them know when she saw Marta's family coming. Right about time for supper, Michael saw them walking toward the house. She ran into the house and alerted everyone, to which Hadiza bemoaned, "We are not ready, oh my, we are not ready! I knew this would happen. How embarrassing."

Marta looked at her and said, "Will you relax? If anything is not finished, my mother and sisters-in-law will help. Just relax and enjoy yourself and stop worrying so much."

Marta's family arrived full of excitement over the news of the baby. The food was not quite ready, and Marta's mother and two sisters-in-law rolled up their sleeves and jumped right in to help. Hadiza was mortified—that is, until Marta's mother came over, put her arm around her, and hugged her and asked how she was doing, treating her as if she was one of her sisters. Now, finally, Hadiza understood why Marta treated all the servants like family; it was the way she had been raised. In her house, while Marta was growing up, her mother treated everyone that lived in the house as if they were family, so it came naturally to Marta.

"Where is Saana?" asked her father.

Marta responded, "We have not seen him today. He is probably out in the fields, or in one of the barns tending to one of the animals. Anyway, I do not believe he will be dining with us tonight."

With the last statement, she heard a giggle from Michael. Marta gave her a firm look that stopped the giggling immediately.

Unseen from the house was Saana standing in the shadows beside one of the barns. He watched as all of Marta's family arrived, and after last night, he was sure any time now the father and his two sons would come looking for him. He was torn between hiding or running. Terrified, he reasoned, "What do I do? I was such fool last night. I seem to keep digging myself into a hole deeper and deeper."

"What happened to your arm?" one of the field hands asked. Saana was holding his swollen arm next to his body, and the field worker could see the bruises. "Oh, I had a little accident feeding the animals." He lied. Saana was repeating to himself over and over, "What is she telling them? What are they saying? Is that her father leaving the house?" Then he realized it was just a shadow. "I need to run, but where would I go? That was so stupid of me last night, just so stupid. I was so angry at her I wanted to kill her. Oh, how I wanted to kill her. What was I thinking? She won. Oh, how I hate that woman. She won. She won again! Oh, by the gods how I hate that woman!"

Now depression was taking the place of Saana's anger. He walked back to his temporary room and laid on his makeshift bed and poured himself a cup of wine both to sooth his nerves and numb the pain in his arm. Muttering to himself, "I keep trying to win this battle of wills against her, and each time, my situation gets worse. Something has to change. Either I surrender or I keep sleeping in the barn and hiding from her family, waiting for the day they think I crossed some line and then I am a dead man. Something has got to change." He dropped the cup and picked up a wine skin full of wine and slowly sipped from the wine skin as he the contemplated his situation and was soon fast asleep.

By the time Saana pulled himself out of bed, the sun had already been up for a couple of hours. He was surprised the rooster crowing hadn't awakened him. The night before last, he didn't get much sleep from the pain. His arm throbbed from the blows Lo and Gamal had delivered. It wasn't broken, but it hurt horribly. He figured a combination of the lack of sleep and the wine helped him sleep through the night. He went over to a basin already full of water, filled by one of his field hands. He washed his face and got dressed. He had something special he had to do today. He thought it out last night and, with a cool and sober head, came to realize there was only one answer to his situation and he was going to act on that answer today. So with quick, deliberate steps, he walked over to the house—to swallow his pride. He knocked on the door, and Hadiza's daughter Misam answered it and called her mother over to the door. "What can I do for you, master?" Hadiza asked with a rather sour tone in her voice.

Saana ignored her tone and said, "You can call your mistress to the door. I need to speak with her. I come in peace. I have no stick or other weapon with me. I just need to talk with her. You can call for Lo and Gamal as well, just to make sure I can do no harm." The last part he said sarcastically with his now toothless smile.

Marta and Gamal came to the door. Gamal was a bit cautious, but Marta opened the door wide with her arms crossed and with a stern voice said, "What do you want I'm not really in the mood for trouble from you this morning, I'm not feeling very well."

Saana raised his hand up to chest level with his palm facing Marta, dropped his head, and said, "You win—I will say it again, you win. In my efforts to bring you down and humble you, I have lost my bed. I have lost control of my house. My own house! I have lost the fear and respect of the household servants and gained the ire and hatred of your family, which may someday get me killed. I never should have married you, but I did and now we are stuck with each other. I propose a truce, a better living arrangement for everyone. I propose that I move back to my bedroom. I promise never to interfere in the household affairs, and I promise never to touch you again. For good or ill, I will never touch you or any of your servants again. We will live separate lives, except where custom demands and, even then, with a great amount of latitude. You win. I say again, you win. I will never bother you again. You have my word. Is this acceptable?"

Marta stared at Saana for a moment, looked down, and then looking him in the eye, said, "This is acceptable to me. But let me warn you. I have no patience with you anymore. You touch me or my servants again, and it will be my life's mission to see you pay a very dear price indeed. I will carry out my promise then for sure. I have instructed the servants to treat you with respect, and if any of them get out of line with you, let me know. But you don't touch them, understand? Also, if you get out of line with the servants, I will let you know in no uncertain terms. Get out of line with me, and my family will let you know. Do you understand?"

Saana stared her straight in the eyes and quietly said, "I understand and agree to your terms. So can I move back to my room in the house or not? It's terrible sleeping in the barn. I didn't build this house to sleep in the barn. So whatever it takes, I will do."

Marta looked at the servants, as all of them had gathered around by now, and for one additional humiliation factor, she looked around at their faces and said, "Your master has agreed to be civil from this day forward. He has agreed to never interfere in the household affairs, and he has agreed to never raise his voice or strike any of you ever again. Isn't that right, husband?" The last part she said in an effort to rub in that one last humiliation.

Saana, looking down, said, "Yes, that is the agreement I have proposed, and I hope that your mistress accepts my proposal." He winced as he tried to move his injured arm, and everyone noticed, which made him feel even more awkward. He looked exhausted, and the fire in his eyes had gone out. He had truly been beaten.

Marta said, "Then under those conditions, I accept your offer. You may move back in immediately, and Gamal and Lamel will help you."

"What about Lo?" the words came out of Saana's mouth before he realized it and he knew it was a mistake.

Marta looked at him with a long, hard, stone-cold stare and said, "I have other things for Lo to do."

She then smiled and turned her back on Saana in a way that is insulting in their culture.

Saana cursed himself for asking about Lo and almost ruining all the pride swallowing and humiliation he had just endured. He was back in his house and was able to retain a small amount of his dignity. He declared to himself that he would never make that mistake again. "Keep your mouth shut, you fool, keep your mouth shut." He then led Gamal and Lamel to the barn where he had been sleeping, and they helped him move back into his bedroom in less than an hour. Saana stayed in his room for the rest of the day. Marta had Hadiza bring him his meals of which he ate very little. The next morning, Saana was out in the fields as if nothing had happened.

9

A Dream Lives and Dies

Months went by without incident. Saana kept to his word and left Marta and the household staff alone. As was his prior custom, he ate his meals in his room or in the courtyard and spent the rest of his day in the fields or in one of the barns.

Weeks went by, and Saana nether talked to Marta or the servants at all. Marta was eight months into her pregnancy and vacillated between joy and all consuming worry. Every time she felt the baby kick, she was worried that something was wrong, and the baby kicked frequently. When the baby didn't kick, she worried even more. Hadiza tried to comfort her and reassure her. "Marta, the baby is fine. It's normal for them to move or stay quiet for a while. You are fine. The backache and being nervous is normal. Just breathe. Take a deep breath and just breath. Everything is going to be fine."

Marta smiled; this sounded funny coming from Hadiza—Hadiza the worrier. But it was hard for Marta to feel assured. This was her dream child. Her life's dream. She dreamed about having children since she was thirteen, and if Saana had anything to say about it, this was going to be her one and only chance at that the dream would become a reality. She reached out and took Hadiza's hand, "I can't relax.There are so many things that can go wrong. My mind keeps going to the what ifs. What if there is something wrong with me that would affect the baby? What if I do something that would hurt the baby? I'm just so scared."

Hadiza looked Marta in the eyes and said, "I will watch out for you. I won't let anything happen to you or the baby. Trust me. I have

91

two daughters, and it all turned out well with them, it will for you as well."

Marta took a deep breath and exhaled the words, "I'll try."

Hadiza patted her on the hands and reiterated, "You'll be okay. Do you hear me? You'll be okay."

Marta's family was almost more excited about the baby than Marta was, if that was possible. They had a large party, and it seemed like they had invited half the town. There was a lot of congratulating, many hugs and tears of joy. For Marta, it was both an enjoyable time and a tough time as well. Of course, Saana never came to the celebration, but no one seemed to notice, or at least they never mentioned him or asked about him. It was as if he never existed.

The last month of her pregnancy passed quickly, though for Marta, it seemed like a lifetime. Then one day, while she was standing in the kitchen helping with supper, she felt a strange sensation and realized her water had broken. She nearly went into a panic. "Hadiza! Is everything okay? What happened? Is the baby okay? I'm scared!" Hadiza took her by the hand and led her to her room and directed Michael to fetch the midwife and instructed Marta to get undressed and get into bed. "Everything is all right. We are about to meet the little one you have been carrying around all these past months. You are about to meet your baby face-to-face in just a little while."

The midwife arrived breathless and full of excitement. She immediately shooed everyone out of the room, but Hadiza and started working on Marta. The labor lasted about six hours, with the last two hours being hard labor. Marta kept asking repeatedly how the baby was.

When the baby was born, the midwife shouted out so the whole house could hear, "It's a boy! Marta, you have a son." Even Saana who was in the courtyard heard the midwife shouting and felt both deflated and yet, somewhere deep inside, a little sense of pride, though he would never admit it in a million years. He turned and went back to his fields, grumbling to himself.

The midwife washed the baby boy and wrapped him in a soft blanket and handed him to his mother. "Congratulations, you are the mother of a healthy baby boy. I'm so happy for you. Do you want me to tell your family? Your mother and I have been friends since childhood. It would be a joy to see her face when she finds out you had a boy. And your father, oh my, he will be dancing with joy."

Marta said, "Please tell them and have them come right away. I want to show them their grandson, their beautiful grandson." With that, the midwife ran off to Marta's family home and, when she arrived shouted from the door, "She had a boy, Marta had a boy!" From inside the house, there came a scream and the sound of a bowl falling to the floor.

In less than an hour, her whole family showed up at Marta's house breathless as if they had run the whole way. Her mother was streaming tears, and her father was beside himself with joy, clapping his hands and patting everyone he saw on the shoulder. He hugged everyone and laughed and hugged some more. "This is the happiest day of my life!" he shouted over and over. He had six other grandchildren, but this one was the miracle child.

Everyone wanted to hold the baby, and this started to make Marta extremely nervous. She finally said with a loud voice that her mother and father were the only ones allowed to hold the baby. With that, the enthusiasm dampened, but they all understood.

Her father asked, "What is his name? Has Saana given him a name? It was customary for the father to name the baby."

Lo responded, "Gamal had looked for him, but Saana was nowhere to be found."

Marta's father was extremely perturbed and decided to take it upon himself to name the baby. He stood up and looking rather officious declared, "He shall be called Elisha after the prophet that predicted his birth. We can call him Eli, and if there is any dissension about the name from the neighbors, so what! We owe the prophet some honor, and I cannot think of a better way to honor him."

All in the room agreed and were eager to see how the prophet would react to the news. Marta smiled and in a quiet voice said, "Perfect, just perfect. I will call him Eli, and I will proudly argue with anyone who would prefer a Shunammite name. Eli is perfect."

She looked down at the baby and said, "From this day forward, and for the rest of your life, you will be known as Elisha, son of Saana."

The celebrating went on for two hours until finally, Hadiza said, "Enough, she has had enough celebrating. She is tired. You all realize she has just had a baby. No easy task, wouldn't you agree?" Everyone in the room laughed and quietly started to leave. Marta's mother gave the baby and her daughter one more kiss and then, without saying a word, left to catch up with the rest of the family.

The next day, Saana came to Marta's room, with Lo and Gamal close behind, and asked for permission to see the baby. The minute he saw the child, he knew it was his for sure and didn't say a word. He never even asked what the child's name was. He just turned around and went to the large barn, looking defeated.

Lo stayed behind and asked, "What is next now that you have the child? How are you going to handle Saana? I still don't trust that man." Marta thought for a minute before she answered and said, "I believe Saana will just continue to live his life separate form all of us. I don't believe he will try anything again. He's lost the war, and he knows it. I would be surprised if he actually has anything to do with his son. That is too bad, though, a boy needs his father."

Lo replied, "Gamal and I will be the men in his life. Unless something happens to Saana, and you marry again." Marta looked a little sad then took in a deep breath and smiled and said, "That's not likely to happen. Saana will die eventually for sure, but as for me marrying again, I don't think so. I think I've had enough of marriage for this lifetime."

"I understand, I completely understand," Lo said with a tender smile.

*****

The next six years passed with Marta raising Eli mostly without a father's assistance. Saana would only grunt when the child said hello to him, that was the extent of their father-son relationship. Lo and Gamal stepped in as father role models, and Lamel treated Eli as though he were his younger brother. The female servants fussed over him like they were his aunts. Marta's family were over quite often and would have the boy and his mother stay overnight with them once or twice a month. The boy was surrounded with a loving and nurturing family. But sadly, Eli was deeply fascinated with his father. Even though his father completely ignored him, Eli tried just that much harder to get his father's attention.

At six years old, Eli was curious about what his father did during the day. The boy asked his mother if he could go out and watch his father work in the fields. She was hesitant; he kept asking and she finally gave in, "But only if Lo goes with you." Eli was elated. He and Lo went hand in hand to the wheat field where his father was plowing with several of the field servants. Eli shouted out to Saana, but his father, with a nod of his head, only passively acknowledged his presence. Eli was unperturbed. He was just excited to see all that his father did. He loved watching the oxen pulling the plows and his father and the servants managing the oxen. To him as a six-year-old boy, it looked like they were playing a great big game, he was excited about every move they made.

Eli and Lo watched his father work for about an hour when the boy started to complain about his head hurting. Saana came over to get a drink of water,and Eli with tears in his eyes and said, "Father, my head hurts, my head hurts really bad."

Saana looked at the boy then at Lo, and with a disgusted tone in his voice, he said, "Take the boy to his mother. I don't have time for a whinny boy underfoot."

Eli responded with tears, "I'm sorry. I won't complain anymore. Let me stay. I want to watch. Please let me stay. I promise I won't get in the way. Please?"

Lo looked at the boy and realized he was in considerable pain and said, "No, we will go to your mother for now. We will come back out later once you start feeling better."

Eli pleaded, "You promise. Do you promise we can come back out?"

Lo looked him in the eye and said, "I promise. Come, let's go and see your mother."

With that, Lo took Eli's hand and started to walk back to the house when Eli asked if Lo could carry him. It was unusual for the very independent Eli to ask to be carried, and it disturbed Lo very much. Lo picked him up and carried him across the field to the house at a faster pace. Marta, who had been keeping an eye out for them, saw them returning and then saw that Lo was carrying the boy to the door, which was strange. When they got closer, she saw the look on Lo's face and knew something was seriously wrong.

With a nervous voice, she asked, "What's wrong? Is Eli okay? Why are you carrying him?"

Lo explained, "He started to complain about his head hurting, and his father ordered me to bring Eli to you. I think he is very sick. He complained that his head was hurting worse, and he asked me to carry him back."

"Here, give him to me," Marta said tenderly, fear gripping her throat.

She took the boy, and as soon as she did, she realized he was awfully sick indeed. There was no fever, but his eyes looked hollow, and she could tell he was struggling to stay awake. A wave of fear overwhelmed her. She looked at Lo with pleading eyes, and Lo just looked down.

"Do you want me to fetch the physician?" Lo asked, trying to help, but he already knew that the town physician was completely ineffectual and having him try to help was probably worse than doing nothing; as Gamal would say, "He's as worthless as a monkey waving a feather."

Marta, with a sad note in her voice, responded, "No. You know as well as I do that his condition is serious. I will hold Eli and help him as much as I can. Come, big boy, let's go into the courtyard and watch the birds. They are especially noisy this morning."

Marta carried her son over to a chair in the courtyard and sat down and held him in her lap. Eli was whimpering and would cry out in pain occasionally, complaining that the pain in his head was terrible and getting worse. His mother rocked him back and forth, trying to comfort him as much as she could. She had Michael bring a damp cloth that she could put on his head and neck, trying to help, but without much success. When he cried, she would kiss him on the head and sing him a children's song.

It was midmorning, and the birds filled the trees that surrounded the house and courtyard. She would try to distract him by pointing out different birds and tell him again the story about the angel that came to her room a long time ago. He loved that story, and while she told it, he tried to smile, however weak. Eli moaned and started to cry again. As the morning wore on, he cried less, and his whimpering stopped. In a normal situation, this might be taken as a good sign, but Marta, with a mother's intuition, knew that Eli was losing his battle. She felt so helpless. Soon, there was no crying at all.

Marta gasped, "Oh, Eli, my Eli!" With her heart painfully burdened, she mumbled in a desperate sigh, "No, no, this can't be happening. Why is this happening? Prophet, where are you? I need you now more than ever before!"

Overtaken in grief, she started to tear up but realized that if anyone knew that this was fatal, they might want to bury him right away, and she couldn't have that. If they buried him, then there would be no hope at all. It couldn't end this way—it just couldn't. There had to be a way to save her son.

Shortly before noon, Eli's breathing became shallow, and he was not responding to her. He became limp, and his breathing became shallower and shallower. "Breathe, son, just breathe," she pleaded quietly. "Please breathe. Oh, God of Elisha, don't take him from me, please, please!" She caressed his hair and kissed his cheek and repeated, "Please just keep on breathing, little one, and then it will be all right. Please, just breathe." She rocked back and forth with him and gently caressed his hair. She felt no panic, just a painful realization that she was losing her son—that he was slipping away from her. Her dream was dying, and she was helpless to stop it. She looked at her little boy in the face. It was empty of color. She knew it was over. He had stopped breathing. Her son had slipped away. Her dream had just died. Everything she lived for lay lifeless in her lap. Marta was numb. She didn't cry out; she couldn't cry out—just a few tears slid down her cheek. She sat there for about an hour holding him. She was in shock. Her stare was blank and as lifeless as her son's body.

She looked down on his face and said, "Your pain has stopped, little one. If I could just die with you, then the pain would stop for me too." Suddenly, a tiny sparrow landed next to her and just stared at her as if to say something. She thought, *Strange, this little bird is not afraid of me at all.* She spoke to the bird and said, "There is hope. I know that this is crazy, but I still have hope. I refuse to believe that there is no hope." Somewhere deep inside of her, somewhere in her innermost being, she sensed a spark of life welling up and whispering to herself said, "Breathe, Marta, just breathe. Take a breath. Come on, breathe!"

She drew in a deep breath and started to feel life awaken in her spirit. Her head was swimming, but for the first time in an hour, she was feeling something; she was no longer numb. Her few tears stopped, and she looked around, and no one else was in the courtyard except that little bird, and just as quickly as it came, it turned and flew off. She tried to think, to reason the situation out, but her pain was so great that it was drowning out all sense of reason. She was fighting to hold on to any sense of sanity. She had no direction on what to do next. She felt truly lost. She whispered, "What do I do? What can I do? I know there is something I can do. It can't end like this. It can't. I need to get up and do something. What can I do?"

Slowly, as she took a few more deep breaths, her head started to clear, and an idea started to formulate; a plan started to come together. She stood up with the boy in her arms and headed to the prophet's room. She prayed that no one would see her and think she was a crazy woman and then, worst of all, take the child from her. As she started to walk, a resoluteness came over her. She now knew exactly what she needed to do, and no one was going to stop her, no one. She could not, would not, allow her son to be buried. The custom in Shunem was to bury the dead before the sun went down, and she was not about to allow that to happen.

She looked around and whispered again, "No one would dare go into the prophet's room, that's where I'll put him. He'll be safe there. No one will disturb him in the prophet's room. No one would dare." She carried the child to the room on the rooftop. She opened the door and walked in and laid the dead child on the prophet's bed. "Sleep now, my little one, I'm going for help. No one will bother you here. So just you sleep until mother gets back." She brushed his cheek one more time and kissed him on the forehead. She quickly turned around and went out of the room, closing the door behind her.

As she walked through the house, she ran into Lo, and he asked how Eli was doing, and she responded, "It is well. Would you please tell Lamel I need to see him right away?" Lo was disturbed by the empty manner Marta talked, but since there were no tears, and she didn't seem shaken, he assumed that the boy was all right and was resting and she was tired herself. Marta went to Saana in the field, and when he saw her, he was immediately upset. "What do you want? I thought we had an agreement. You stay in your world, and I will stay in mine."

She stood erect and said, "Yes, husband, we have an agreement, but it would be unseemly for me to take a trip without your approval. So I came to ask if it was all right for me to go and see the prophet."

Saana snapped back, "Why would you want to go see him? There is no new moon now, and there are no holy days happening right now. Why would you want to go see the prophet?" His son's distress never even came into his thoughts. Saana was completely oblivious that his son might be in some danger, nor did he care.

She responded with all the strength she had to muster. "It is well. I just have a question for him."

Saana waved his hand and said, "Go ahead. What do I care? Is there someone going with you?" The only reason he asked was for appearances' sake. It would be unseemly for a rich man's wife to be seen traveling without an escort.

Marta asked, "If it is all right, I'd like to take Lamel. He would be my escort."

"Good, good. He is young and strong and can offer some protection if you should run into trouble on the road. Go and do whatever it is you feel you need to do, just leave me out of it." He turned and headed toward the barns.

Marta headed back to the house and found Lamel in the kitchen. She instructed him to bring one of the sturdiest donkeys and bring its saddle and instructed him that she would saddle the donkey herself. He was a bit confused about the last part of her command; he always saddled the donkey, but he did as she wished as fast as he could. He did everything "as fast as he could," and that's one of the reasons

Marta chose him to go with her to Mt. Carmel because it's a good day and a half hard ride from Shunem, and she wanted to get there fast. Lamel was young, strong, and would hold up best in a long trip.

He brought the sturdiest and fastest donkey they had. Marta quickly saddled it and handed the bridle to Lamel. She loved Lamel but didn't trust him to saddle it properly, he always tried to hurry through everything he did, and this trip was too important. She sinched the saddle tight but not too tight as to hurt the donkey. As soon as she was done, she looked Lamel straight in the eye and said with a deadly serious voice, "Now I am going to ride this donkey, and I want you to lead him. I want to get to Mt. Caramel as fast as possible, so I don't want you saying hello to anyone. I don't even want you to acknowledge them. Do you understand? Do not greet them in any way at all, do you understand? Just get me there with all possible speed."

Lamel was getting a little uncomfortable with the way Marta was giving him these instructions. She sounded so harsh and demanding. She rarely talked to him like this, and if she did, it was because he was in some deep trouble. "Am I in trouble?" he asked with trepidation.

"No," she said, trying to be a little gentler. "I just need to get there as soon as possible, and I need you to know how important this is to me. Do you understand?"

Lamel nodded and said, "I understand. I will get you there by noon tomorrow. We will ride all night. I will get you there as fast as I can."

They had gotten no further than to the edge of their property, and they ran into the town's head midwife. Lamel started to greet her and looked at Marta and saw quickly how serious she was about ignoring everyone and pressing on to see the prophet. For the rest of the trip, he kept quiet—quiet, that is, except the one time he asked why they were going to see the prophet and was met with silence.

Much of the road was nothing more than a rough trail, rough, dry, and dusty. It was hot, and he was getting exceedingly tired, and his feet were beginning to hurt, but he pushed hard to get there before noon the next day. They pressed on through the night, and Lamel and the donkey were becoming exhausted, and both were stumbling at the smallest imperfection in the road. The only stops were for water at the occasional farmers' well or town center. They reached the base of Mt. Carmel just before noon the next day as Lamel had promised. Marta was exhausted herself, but on getting there, she would be only half done with her journey.

10

Hope Lives

Elisha was standing on the porch of his house, looking out at the view and praying when he saw someone moving up the mountain trail about a half mile away. He squinted and realized it was a woman on a donkey being led by a man. He said, "What in the world are these people up to? There is nothing on this mountain except this house." He squinted again, and this time, he recognized the woman and called out to Gehazi who was standing nearby, "Gehazi, it is that Shunammite woman, Marta? I wonder what she is up to. Go down and ask her if everything is all right. Ask her if her husband and the child are all right." Gehazi was curious as well. He hurried down the road toward the woman and, in ten minutes, met up with her and Lamel.

He stepped in front of them and said, "Good day, Marta. We were on the front porch of the house and were surprised to see you. Is everything all right? My master wants to know if everything is all right with your husband and the child?"

She looked at him with an empty look and smiled an unenthusiastic smile and said, "It is well, thank you. Is it all right if I came up and talked to the prophet? It's been a while since we have seen him in town."

Gehazi was baffled; why would she come all this way? It must be something more important than just checking on the well-being of the prophet. But he gured the only way to nd out was to take her there and see what she wanted. He shrugged his shoulders and said, "Follow me, and I will take you to him."

As they came up the mountain trail to Elisha's house, they were greeted by several of Elisha's students. They had heard of this amazing woman through stories Gehazi shared with them. She was every bit as beautiful and stately as he said she was. They came to the front of the house, and Elisha stepped out to greet Marta. She looked tired, but she was beyond tired; she was completely spent. Elisha raised his hand and said through Gehazi, "Hello, mistress, how is it with you and your family?"

She slid off the donkey and slowly walked over to the prophet and dropped to her face on the ground and grabbed him by his ankles. Her actions caught both Lamel and Gehazi totally by surprise. She cried out, "How could you do this to me? Did I ask a child of you? I didn't, I didn't. How could you allow me to be crushed like this?" Then the tears started to ow in torrents. For the first time, she allowed herself to cry, and she began to weep convulsively. A deeply sad, mourning sound. It sounded as if her very soul was being torn in two.

Gehazi went to pull her away from Elisha and Elisha put out his hand and said, "Stop! She is in deep pain and the Lord has hidden it from me."

He turned to Lamel and said through Gehazi, "Is there a problem with the child?" Lamel stood with his eyes wide and mouth open and simply shook his head.

Marta shouted, "He is dead! Don't you understand? The child you promised me is dead! You have hurt me more than Saana could ever hurt me. I trusted you! I trusted you! Against all odds I believed in you. How could you do this to me?" Gehazi was interpreting as fast as he could. She started to convulse again into a series of deep wailing sobs. Elisha looked at her and could see how exhausted she was. The donkey was on the verge of collapsing, and Lamel looked worse than either Marta or the donkey.

Elisha said to Gehazi, "Ask her. Where is the boy right now?"

She looked up and said, "Tell him he is on the bed in the prophet's room at my house." He looked at Gehazi and handed him his staff. "Go now and lay this staff on the face of the child. Run, and do not stop for anything. If someone greets you, ignore them. Go and take nothing with you. Come, my poor woman, and rest yourself." He ordered one of the students to take care of Lamel and to another student to take care of the donkey.

Marta stood up and said, "I will not rest while my son is in Shunem. Please come to Shunem with me." The prophet didn't understand her words but perceived the heart of what she was saying. Elisha saw that Gehazi had already taken off in a dead run and that she could never keep up, especially in her current state. He looked at her with tender eyes and said, "Gehazi will take care of the child." She looked at Elisha with cold, lifeless eyes and replied, "If you don't go, I will stay here. I will not leave this place. Without my son, I am a dead woman, and I will have you bury me on this mountain. If you don't go, neither will I. There is nothing left for me in life without my son. I will die here."

Elisha looked at her, again understanding her heart and intent, took a deep breath, and ordered another student to saddle his mule and put her on it. He said, "I am going to Shunem and let her servant know where we have gone as soon as he is rested. He can return home whenever he feels strong enough. Give him provisions and send him with his donkey when he is ready." The prophet and his servant helped Marta onto the saddle, and Elisha climbed up behind her to keep her from falling off if she fell asleep. He gave the mule a nudge, and the mule started at a trot. Elisha could tell that Marta was not going to be able to stay awake long, so he wrapped his cloak around her to help keep her in place. Within half a mile, she was fast asleep, sitting up wrapped tightly in the prophet's cloak.

Lamel was already sleeping soundly in the great room. He still had a mouthful of food and was lying on his side on three pillows. The donkey was being brushed and tended and was looking better already.

Gehazi ran through several small villages and was greeted by a few people whom he simply ignored, not even looking in their direction. He stopped at a few wells for water and was now regretting not taking any food with him. It was hot and dusty, but he pressed on at a rhythmic pace. He was already halfway to Shunem before he knew it. He was stirred by his master's trust in him, sending him instead of any of a dozen students who had been with Elisha far longer than he had. He didn't want to let his master down. At noon the next day, he saw Shunem at a distance and picked up his pace, which had been a fast trot. He was soon in the town and ran into his father in the street. His father was extremely upset when he called out to his son and his son ignored him, keeping his intent on one purpose—to ful ll the master's command.

He arrived at Marta's house and immediately ran to the prophet's room and saw the boy laying on the bed. He half stumbled and half ran up to the child and carefully placed the prophet's staff on the boy's body with the top of the staff on his face. It wasn't until then he suddenly realized he had no idea what to do next. He stood there perplexed. "What do I do now? I don't know what to do!" He stepped out of the room and looked up and prayed, "Yahweh, God of Elisha, I don't know what to do next! Sis is terrible, I don't know what to do! Elisha makes it look so easy. How I wish he had come instead of sending me. Help me, Yahweh."

He went into the room again and saw that nothing had happened. He went over to the boy's body, shook him, and yelled, "Live, boy live I say! By the God of Elisha, I command you to live!" Still nothing. Gehazi went over to one of the chairs and put his face in his hands and started to cry. His master sent him,he had trusted him, and he failed. He had seen his master heal many people and at the same time put to shame many priests of Baal, but here, Gehazi felt helpless. He couldn't do anything. He simply was at a loss as to what to do next.

He sat there for nearly an hour and finally said to himself, "I must go back and tell my master it didn't work. To let him know that I failed." He left the staff on the boy in hopes that something may happen, then he left the room and closed the door behind him. He was relieved that none of the servants had noticed him coming to the house, so he didn't have to stop and explain what he was doing. He started in a slow trot back to his master, but he had run out of endurance; and with hunger, fatigue, and lack of success, he was having trouble even walking, let alone running. Gehazi did a stumbling trot for about an hour when he saw his master in the distance, riding his mule but something was a little off. Elisha had his cloak around something in front of him. Soon he saw the legs of someone besides the prophet beneath the cloak and realized it was Marta.

Elisha rode up to Gehazi and asked, "How is the child?"

Gehazi looked down and said, "I laid the staff on the child, and nothing happened. I didn't know what else to do. I'm sorry, I failed. I failed" as he kept his gaze toward the ground.

Elisha smiled and said, "No, my son, I was wrong to send you. I was concerned for the lady, and instead of sending you I should have gone myself. It was not for you to do, it was my task, not yours. You did well. Look at me." Gehazi looked Elisha in the eyes. "You did well. When we are done here, I want you to go to your father's house and rest. You must be exhausted. You can then get some food and some rest. But for now, you and I have a task to do."

With that, the prophet prompted the mule to move on, and they came to the house in about forty minutes. He shook the shoulders of Marta and woke her up. She was groggy and a little confused. She slept nearly the whole way. Elisha was impressed and thought it was quite a feat to sleep while sitting on a trotting mule. They went into the prophet's room and saw the boy lying just as Gehazi had left him, with the staff still laying on the child. He sent Marta down into the house where her servants were surprised to see her.

Lo asked, "Where have you been? We were worried about you. Where is Lamel? Where is your son? Did you go to see the prophet? We went to yourparents' house and told them we were looking for you and now they are worried as well." Then they saw Elisha's mule and understood he was in his room. Very exhausted physically, emotionally, and spiritually, Marta, silently stared into the distance, walked over to the fountain, and collapsed.

Elisha walked over to the boy and ordered Gehazi to close the door. He then lifted his staff off the boy and crawled onto the bed and laid on the child faceto-face, with his hands on the boy's hands. Gehazi was baffled and thought to himself, *What is he doing? I have never seen him do this before. Is this what I was supposed to do?* Elisha laid on the child for about ve minutes, got up, left the room, and went down into the house. The servants watched as he walked back and forth for about ve minutes and then went back to the room and laid back on the child again, face-to-face, hands to hands. He laid on the child for five minutes again and again went down into the house. He repeated this seven times.

Gehazi was growing more perplexed with each time they returned to the room and thought to himself, "When is he just going to give up? This is the seventh time he has gone and laid on the boy, and nothing has happened." The seventh and last time that Elisha went up and laid on the boy, he whispered something, and the child sneezed, then he sneezed again and again, sneezing seven times in all. Elisha got off the bed and sat the child on the edge of the bed and told Gehazi who stood dumbfounded, "Go and fetch his mother."

Gehazi was frozen in fascination. Elisha said louder and, with a little irritation in his voice, "Gehazi! Go fetch the boy's mother now!" Gehazi suddenly realized his master was talking to him and ran out to get Marta. When Gehazi came into the courtyard, he saw Marta staring into thin air, and he said with a loud voice, "Lady, my master summons you. He has news for you." He tried to hold in his excitement, but Marta wouldn't have noticed anyway; she was almost catatonic. With shuffling steps, she followed him through the house and up to the prophet's room. She went in, almost unseeing. Lo and the other servants followed and stood at the door looking in, mysti ed as to what was going on.

When Marta saw Eli sitting on the edge of the bed, smiling, she blinked several times. She looked over at the prophet and back to her son. It took her a minute to move anything but her head. The prophet said, "Tell her to pick up her son." Gehazi was expecting her to cry out, run over, and pick up the boy, but then she did something totally unexpected. She turned to the prophet, dropped to her knees, grabbed the bottom of his robe, and with tears in her eyes and head bowed, she said, "Thank you." She then stood up and walked over to her son, picked him up, and hugged him so tightly that he grunted out, "Mother, you're hurting me. I can't breathe." She then loosened her hug and started to cry. She kept kissing him all over his face and head.

The other servants couldn't gure out what was going on, so Gehazi took them aside and explained all that had happened. The servants were amazed. How could they not know that such a terrible thing had happened and then witness such a wonderful thing right before their eyes? Their admiration for Marta grew exponentially. The strength it took to keep her head was incredible. A murmur went through them as they suddenly understood that if they had known then Saana would have found out and he would have had the boy buried before an hour had passed. Thank God they didn't know, and even more so, that Saana never found out.

They watched in wonder as Marta carried her son out of the prophet's room and down into the house. Eli complained that he was hungry, and Hadiza immediately ran and got some of his favorite foods. Raisin cakes, honey cakes, and dates. The boy was excited about seeing all the food but was confused about why his mother let him eat these sweet foods so close to lunch. He had no recollection of the events that had transpired over the last three days. Marta laughed and started hugging the boy all over again. Her dream was back; it was a little boy, and he was alive. Her dream was back with her again. Life was worth living again.

As for Saana, he was standing in the middle of one of his wheat fields, and his head field servant, Ishaman, came and told Saana what he heard about Eli dying and being brought back to life again by the hand of Elisha. He plopped down in the middle of the eld and yelled out in frustration. First, that he didn't even know about the child's death, and then he was even more infuriated about his resurrection. His heart was so hard that even his own son's death was to him only another opportunity for revenge on Marta, and now that was taken away from him. His hatred for her was all-consuming. Then Saana, with a cold heart, blackened with pain suddenly clutched his chest and, in a breathless rage, looked up to the sky and screamed at the God of Elisha, "You robbed me of my revenge again!" He shook his st in the air and then crumpled to the ground.

Ishaman, Saana's chief field servant, found Saana dead, lying on his back in the middle of the wheat field. Ishaman just stood there for a few minutes staring at the pathetic figure of a man whose dead eyes were staring blankly at the sky. No remorse, no sadness, just a benign contempt for the corpse of a man who made him and his fellow servants' lives so miserable. Such marks the death of a man like Saana—empty, with only one to morn his passing, with only one that would sincerely miss him—his son.

They buried Saana before dark that day with minimal ceremony. To his servants, it was just one more matter-of-fact chore that needed to be done before the day was over. As the last shovel of dirt was thrown over the grave, Marta sighed while Eli cried.

PART 2
2 Kings 8:1–6

11
A Famine Is Coming

Five years had passed since Saana's death, and things were as Marta had dreamed they would be when she was sixteen. She had a large house, many servants, a healthy son and the money and freedom to do as she pleased. The learning curve for the business was steep, though. She knew absolutely nothing about farming. She knew very little about livestock and nothing at all about plowing, planting, and harvesting. Immediately after the death of Saana, she sat down with Ishaman, the head field servant, and had Lo and Gamal join them. She appointed Lo to be head over all the household servants. Years ago, Hadiza may have had issues with Lo being in charge, but she had come to a place where she trusted and respected both Lo and especially Marta. Anyway, she had also learned not to challenge Marta on any of these kinds of decisions. Because Gamal knew about farming, Marta had Gamal oversee Ishaman and his field servants, which greatly perturbed the head field servant. She trusted Gamal and didn't know Ishaman. The head field servant was a tall and thin man with straight black hair, a thin drawn face, heavy forehead, and brown, almost black eyes. He was a hard man and lacked any sort of compassion. Maybe Ishaman knew more about farming, but right now, trust was more important than experience to Marta; and she couldn't bring herself to trust the man at all.

There were a few bumps along the way but that only happened when Marta got in the way of one of Gamal or Lo's decisions about planting or marketing the farm products, and she soon learned she knew even less than she originally thought. Now she just wanted

111

to know expenditures and profits, the details she left up to the three people she put in charge. *I need to stick with my expertise and over time learn as much as I can about the rest of the estate's business. I just need to trust them.*

Eli was growing into a ne young man. He was nearly as tall as Lo, had large brown eyes and a full head of very bushy black hair. He had a thin build like his father but at eleven was already more muscular than his father had been as an adult. He was in the fields as often as Marta would allow. She had Lo teaching Eli the art of writing and reading. Ishaman occasionally grumbled about Eli being underfoot, and then she sternly reminded Ishaman that someday Eli would be in charge and that the head field hand could easily be replaced. That seemed to calm the situation and stopped the complaints.

One afternoon, she heard that the prophet had come into town and had turned into his room and was resting. She waited for three hours outside the room until Elisha came out. When he saw her, he smiled a large smile. "Well, mistress, how are you doing on this fine day?"

She stood up and with a mock frown said, "What do you mean turning into your room without first greeting the head of the house?"

He shook his head and said, "I beg your pardon. I was very tired and was a little reluctant to give you bad tidings. My God spoke to me a few days ago and directed me to advise you to leave this region for a while. A famine is coming, and it will be extremely severe. I won't tell you where to go, though I do have a suggestion. Also, you will need to leave for a rather long period of time."

She leaned forward and asked, "How long is the 'long period of time'?"

The prophet looked down and replied, "Seven years."

Marta was shocked and exclaimed, "Seven years! How do I live away from Shunem for seven years? I have the money, but what about my family? How do they get by?"

Elisha ignored her question and said, "Send for your father and have him come, and we will discuss your options."

She sent Michael to fetch her father. "Tell him it's urgent and that the prophet and I need to talk to him right away."

Akeem arrived almost a half an hour later, a bit winded from half walking, half running. The words "The prophet and I need to talk to you" spurred him on.

If her father had a hero in life, it was Elisha. Not only for the birth of his grandson but also for raising him from the dead. He also admired how even kings show deference, if not outright fear, of this legendary prophet of God. The fact that Elisha stayed at his daughter's house on occasion was a great source of pride for him that he bragged about to his friends frequently. The chance to talk with him was exciting and even more exciting is that he asked for him personally. He could barely contain himself.

When Michael escorted him into the house and saw Elisha sitting on some pillows in the dining area, he had a sudden urge to drop to his knees and bow; he refrained. "What can I do for you prophet? I am at your service." The prophet motioned to Akeem to sit with him, which he did in an awkward way, plopping himself a little too close to Elisha, and he quickly slid himself over to a more comfortable distance from the honored guest. Marta was amused at her father's unexpected awkwardness, and evident nervousness at meeting with Elisha in an "official capacity." Yes, he had met Elisha several times before but never because the prophet summoned him. Her father was honored beyond words, and she could see it. It was a little amusing and heartwarming at the same time.

Elisha leaned forward and said, "I have given some disturbing news to your daughter this afternoon. My God has spoken to me to warn her of a famine that is coming, a harsh one. It will last seven years, and I told her she needs to leave the region until the famine is over. She is concerned for all of you as well. So I believe you all need to discuss the situation, and I will give advice whenever it is asked for."

Akeem sat there for a minute trying to take it all in and finally said, "Seven years? That's a long time to abandon your home. What do we do with all our furnishings? We have animals. What do we do with them? Marta has this large farm with many servants and livestock. Do they take them as well? Where do you suggest we all go? What do you suggest we take with us?" He was getting more frustrated the more he spoke.

Marta finally interrupted him, "How soon should we leave? Are we looking at days, weeks, months? What time frame are we looking at?"

Elisha leaned back against a pillar that he had propped some pillows against, he closed his eyes and spoke through Gehazi, "You need to leave before the end of spring. Any seed you plant now will be wasted as there will be no rain this summer, only heat and sun. Take as much grain as you can to help through the first year. This famine will be felt even in Egypt, so grain will be hard to come by after the first year. As for the animals, let Ishaman stay and do the best he can in trying to keep them alive. Some of the animals you can take with you, such as the donkeys and oxen. You can rent them out to farmers or wagon masters at wherever you end up. As for where to go, I suggest Philistia. They are next to the coast, and if there is any rain, they will see it first and see the most. My God has not given me any specific direction for you, but this is a direction that I feel comfortable advising you to go. I can understand your reluctance, but you need to trust me on this."

Elisha leaned forward for emphasis. "Listen, you must trust me on this. If you do not, I see disaster for those who stay. Maybe even to the death. Please, do as I advise. I have come to be very fond of this family and would hate to see any disaster fall upon you. Please trust me."

Marta's father had calmed down. Listening to the prophet, he realized there was a way to make this work, and the prophet's pleading touched him. He understood now that his family was not just people Elisha knew, but that the prophet really was truly concerned for Akeem and his family. Then Akeem spoke up, "I will start sending servants to scout out places in Philistia that would meet our family's needs. We need a house large enough for all of us, family, and servants." He turned to Marta, "Marta, I suggest you talk to Ishaman together with Lo and Gamal to figure out a plan for the next several years. What food to take, what animals to take, what furnishings to take, who will stay and who will go. There is so much to discuss. We are at the end of fall, so we have about four months to be ready."

Elisha nodded and smiled. "Sat is an excellent plan. I believe a port city would be best because you are not so dependent on the rain in a port city. They will import grain and will need large livestock such as oxen for the additional wagons they will be using. It might be easier to find a house on the outskirts of the city you choose. Sending a couple of servants to scout out the region is a great idea and reminiscent of the twelve men Moses sent to spy out the land."

The comparison to Moses was not known or recognized by the Shunammites. They had heard of the name Moses and understood that the Jews revered him, but they didn't know the story about Moses sending out twelve men to spy out land that would become Israel. The rest of his suggestions they understood, and they were in complete agreement with them. Marta called Lo and Gamal in to tell them the situation and have them set up a meeting with Ishaman. They were all taken back by the enormity of the issue. They understood and had faith in the prophet, but the length of time left them uneasy. Lo was the most disturbed and asked, "Once we are settled in Philistia, can we send one of us back at certain intervals to see how things are going? Sat way, if there are problems, either you or your father can come back and intervene."

"I fully agree," said Gamal. "It would take a man on foot about six days travel each way, but I think we would all worry less."

Akeem agreed. "That is wisdom, I believe. We will send someone at regular intervals, probably four times a year. A visit for each season, to bring food, see how it goes with the houses and the livestock. I will have your brothers and their families move into our house. The high wall around the property will offer some protection, and I believe they will need it, you'll see. Now, who do we send to find a city and a house that we can live in? When we find that, we can make more definite plans. We can then look at long-term plans, such as markets and the demand for large livestock. I might be able to continue with my linen and flax business. After all, we are looking for a port city so we can make regular visits to Egypt. This might be a great business opportunity."

Marta thought, *Of course he would be looking at merchant opportunities, he is a natural born businessman. Who knows, we might even get rich there.* Then she smiled at the thought.

Marta cleared her throat. "I believe Lo and Gamal would be the perfect choices. Gamal can assess the house for its potential, and Lo can assess the potential for social, economic, and government issues. No sense in moving to a place that is so unfriendly to foreigners that it would be dangerous to live there."

"Excellent choice," Her father nearly shouted in response. "They both have their strengths, and together, they would be able to determine what would be the right place to settle."

Gamal and Lo glanced at each other with a somewhat distressed look.

Gamal spoke up first. "Is it safe? I heard the Philistines are very unfriendly to strangers. Isn't there another way? To tell the truth, I'm a little afraid about this plan. Is there another way we can do this?"

"They're not so unfriendly anymore," Elisha responded. "Their trade with other countries has caused them to be much more open to strangers, especially in the port cities. They are all thriving with ships of foreign merchandise coming through their ports and them making a lot of money on each shipment. They are unlikely to go out of their way to insult potential sources of money, especially the government won't, and definitely not the king, he has a real love for gold. He will not want to interfere with foreigners if he has a chance to collect taxes from each shipment. And as for your last question, you can stay here and starve or look for a more viable option. No, I think this a great opportunity as well as a good answer to a bad situation."

Lo looked at Gamal again and took a deep breath and nodded. Gamal smiled and nodded back. Gamal responded, "It looks like Lo and I are going to take a little trip to the coast. When do you want us to leave? Better yet, when do want us to be back?" Everyone laughed, and they all looked at Elisha. The prophet responded, "I would leave in a couple of days and be gone no more than forty days. If you want to stay longer, please don't." They all laughed again, and Elisha continued, "I suggest both of you come back and give Akeem an update if you are successful or not, and you all can make any additional decisions from that point."

The two days went by quickly. Early in the morning of the third day Lo and Gamal loaded a donkey with the things they would need for the trip, and they both carried a bag on their staff over their shoulders full of extra food. With tears, Eli begged to go with them, but Marta would have none of it. She lovingly said, "You are only eleven years old. You will have your own adventures soon enough. When you are older, you will have more than enough opportunities for some grand adventures, but not today, my son, not today." Then looking over at Lo and Gamal she said, "But as for you two, I love you like brothers, you take care of yourselves and be careful. I will find it hard to forgive you if you let anything happen to yourselves." She walked over and hugged them both. It was an act that made Lo uncomfortable, but Gamal appreciated the words of concern and hugged her back and tuned and motioned to Lo, and they were on their way.

Lo and Gamal soon faded away in the distance. The whole group watched until both men disappeared around some trees at the last corner, past the city wall. When they were out of view, the household turned and went back into the dwelling.

12
Spying Out the Land

As Lo and Gamal entered Philistine territory, it was as if they had just gone across town. There was almost no difference in the home styles, and there was only a small difference in the style of clothing. It appeared as if they were not even noticed as they walked down the road. They were careful to offer recompense for use of any well they came to, but most refused to take their money. As they got further into Philistia, they noticed the green hills and the abundance of large trees. Occasionally, they saw some men wearing a much different style of clothing, and they appeared to be much wealthier than the other people they saw. The men wore purple robes and red sashes, and they had ornate staffs with gold ornaments on top of the staff. Lo surmised they were priests of some sort as he had seen many priests in Egypt that wore similar robes and sashes. He suggested to Gamal that they give these men a wide berth when passing them along the road.

Lo looked around and quietly said, "I sense trouble when I see these men. Don't look them in the eye and try to not to do anything that would attract their attention. I have seen men like these, and they are trouble wherever they go. They have rules and customs they unreasonably expect you to know, and if you don't follow those laws, the punishment is severe and sometimes fatal. I suspect that these are priests of Baal, and they have a lot of power and influence. I've never seen so many of them in Egypt so watch yourself and keep your guard up."

The whole time they were walking Gamal was surveying the landand assessing the group's ability to travel through to the coast. The roads were well maintained, and there were several fordable streams they had to pass through so there would be plenty of water for the animals when the rest of the group comes. They passed by farm after farm so he surmised that fodder for the animals should be easy to come by.

The barns in Philistia were built differently than in Shunem. In Shunem, the barns were mainly mud brick and stone, and the roofs were at and made of polls, palm fronds, and mud. In Philistia, the barns were made of stone and mortar walls to about eight feet high then were rough beams set side by sidewith an occasional window. The roofs were slopped and made from planks and palm fronds. The houses though were almost identical to the houses in Shunem; mudbrick and stone with flat roofs with six-foot walls surrounding the houses that were outside any city. There were several cities on the route to the coast, and a couple showed some promise, but the prophet suggested that they go to the coast so Lo and Gamal decided they would go as far as Ashkelon and then return to Shunem.

The two men at first avoided staying in the cities, deciding that at night they would get a few hundred yards from the main roads and camp hidden among trees or bushes. Bandits were reported to be numerous along the roads, and they wanted to take no chances. They would cook their meals before it got dark and then put the fire out. The nights were cold and uncomfortable. The cold combined with worrying about bandits made for many sleepless nights. Eventually, they came to realize that they were taking just as great a risk camping in the countryside as they would be staying at an inn in the towns so whenever they came to an inn they would try and stay there. Many of the inns were suspicious of foreigners and would not let them stay. The ones that would let them stay were dirty and rat infested, so the men would mainly stay in the stables with their donkey. It appeared to be safer and somewhat cleaner.

After twelve days, they arrived in the coastal city if Ashkelon. It was a very beautiful port city with wide streets and stone and wood houses. Many of the houses were three and four stories high. None of the houses in Shunem were four stories, and very few were three stories. The city was at least three times as large as Shunem and the population seemed to be ten times larger. Theere were hundreds of fishing boats anchored in the harbor. The aroma of the city got their attention. The smells of fish and the ocean were completely foreign to Gamal. Dozens of large merchant ships were along several docks, breaking the skyline with their tall masts. Unlike Lo, Gamal had never been near the sea and was fascinated. There were dozens of men loading and unloading cargo from the ships with several men standing on the decks of the ships shouting commands to their crews.

Lo instantly recognized several of the crates that were being unloaded. They looked as though they contained Egyptian flax and large bales of cotton. There were also wooden boxes that he was sure contained large bolts of linen. He knew that Marta's father would be excited by this news. Her father probably even knew some of the pilots of the merchant ships and could possibly make business arrangements. Lo was eager to get back and relay this information to Akeem.

As they passed through meandering streets looking for possible places to live that could accommodate all the family and servants, they soon recognized that help from the locals would be necessary. They also realized that people noticed them. Their clothes were different, not a lot different, but different enough to draw some attention. They were thankful, though, that they could better blend in because they could mingle amongst the many sailors from different countries in this seaport city.

They cautiously went into some of the inns both for food and drink but mainly for information. They didn't speak the language, so with some difficulty using their hands and some common words, they asked about the possibility of purchasing a home or property that could be modified into a place where they could all live. After going to three different inns, they found an innkeeper that spoke Egyptian. Lo explained their situation, and the man said he knew of a warehouse near the docks that they might be interested in. He told them that he knew the owner, and the owner was having some financial difficulties and might be willing to negotiate a good price. Because of the confusing directions, the innkeeper gave them it took some intense searching to find the warehouse. His directions had brought them in proximity to the warehouse, but his description of the building was a bit vague. They finally located the warehouse by wandering about, peeking in doors and windows.

It was a large two-story building. The first story was made of stone, and the second was constructed of wood. There were four sets of wide double doors and several large windows on the second floor. One side was located on a dock, and the other side was a busy street full of vendors and other storage facilities and warehouses. There was a constant flow of people and carts passing by the warehouse. It was a very congested and busy area. Lo recognized the area would be excellent for business.

Gamal cautiously peeked into the warehouse from one of the doors that was half open. A large man sitting on a box in the building saw Gamal looking into the building and became instantly angry. He stood up and, in Egyptian, loudly threatened, "What do you want? There is nothing in here to steal, the king saw to that. Leave before I take a stick to you." Gamal didn't understand what the man was saying, but Lo answered back in Egyptian, "We are not thieves. We are servants of a Shunammite woman, and she is looking at moving here for a length of time. We are interested in either renting or buying this building. We wouldn't think of stealing anything. An innkeeper told us the owner might be interested in doing business with us. I'm sorry to hear about your problems with the king. Would these problems prevent you from doing business with us?"

The man looked at them for a few seconds and realizing they were no threat said, "No, none that would prevent us from doing business. As a matter of fact, I might be very interested in doing business. The king wanted taxes I had already paid and took everything I owned to recoup what he thinks I still owed. I paid my taxes, but the tax collector kept most of it and then he complained to the king that I refused to pay. I protested to the king, but he would not listen when I appealed to him for justice, he just accused me of stealing from him. The king ordered that his tax collector confiscate everything I owned except this building. I think the king let me keep my house and this warehouse to be like a thumb in my eye. I am trying to start up my business again, but the other merchants are afraid to do business with me. I'm an Egyptian, and that alone makes doing business difficult. I was a linen merchant, and this warehouse would have dozens of boxes of linens and several bales of cotton at any one time, and now no one will sell me linen or cotton or do any kind of business with me." He started to tear up, which made all three men uncomfortable.

Lo cleared his throat. "I think we can certainly do business with you. As a matter of fact, we may be able to put you back in business, but it will take some time and some trust by my mistress, her father, and on your part."

Looking around and rubbing his chin he said, "Yes, yes, indeed, I think I can see how this is a wonderful opportunity for both of you. My mistress's father is a linen merchant in Shunem and is a rather successful businessman. He has multiple business contacts in Egypt, Judah, Israel, Samaria, and several large cities throughout this part of the world. He may be moving to Ashkelon with my mistress. He has traveled many times to Egypt, so he also speaks Egyptian. Yes, indeed, this may well be a tremendous opportunity for both of you. Are you interested?"

Lo then went over to an empty box and sat down. "By the way, my name is Lo, and this is Gamal, and we are from the city of Shunem. And your name?"

"I am Almed, the owner of this now-empty building. I am originally from a small village in Egypt. I grew up farming cotton and flax, but being the fourth son, I had no prospects of owning my own business. I took what money I inherited and came here to Ashkelon. An old man gave me the idea of opening this business here, and it was all working out well until this last six months." Then Almed became quiet and looked quizzically at Lo, sat down on another box, and started to rub his beard in deep thought.

Almed was a very large man, a full head and a half taller than Gamal, very muscular and broad-chested. He looked like a giant next to Lo. He was bald except for a band of black hair. He had a large black beard that drooped down to his chest. One very noticeable feature about this man that struck Gamal the most was his huge, calloused hands. This man was used to hard work.

Gamal was completely in the dark not understanding a word either man spoke. He knew that somehow, Lo struck a chord on something that got the owner's attention, though he couldn't comprehend what it was. He decided to just stand off to the side and let Lo handle whatever was going on. Wisdom dictated that he didn't have much choice anyway. After a short time of silence, Almed finally turned and looked at Lo and asked, "How is it you speak the Egyptian language? By your manner of speech, I suspect you are from an educated sect of the Egyptian people." Almed leaned forward, studying the men and asked, "Are you spies for Egypt?"

With that, Lo stood up and walked to the door. He turned to Gamal. "It's time for us to leave." Then he turned to Almed and said, "I think you will regret not agreeing with me on my offer. I believe it was an excellent business opportunity and maybe your only option for your financial recovery." Then Lo looked down and said, "Such a shame." He then looked over at Gamal and said, "Let's go."

The warehouse owner jumped up and started to profusely apologize. "I'm sorry, I should have never said that. You have my profound apology. I am a proud man, and I hate feeling fenced in. Forgive me, I'm not thinking clearly. I believe working with your mistress and her father would be help from the gods. I give you my word that I was just reacting out of pressure and frustration. Again, I apologize profusely." Lo saw that he was sincere and sat back down. Almed smiled and relaxed a little, saying, "Come, let's go to my house and talk more and then you can see if it ts your needs. You can stay at my house instead of a rat-infested inn or outside of town with the bandits. I have a very large house with many rooms that could accommodate your mistress and her entire household. As I said, I was very successful until I was betrayed by the king's tax collector. I used to have a lot of servants but had to send most of them away and now I only have three that decided to stay on their own. Please forgive me and accompany me to my house. I will try and make up for my horrible insult."

Lo turned to Almed and, with an irritated huff, replied, "Loose talk like that can be very dangerous for a couple of foreigners like us. What would we be looking for anyway? Trust is a two-way transaction. You need to trust us, and we need to be able to trust you. Any more talk like that and we will have no choice but to leave, not only the waterfront but the city and try to find a place somewhere else."

Then smiling slightly and bowing his head, Lo said, "Now let's leave that in the past. As far as my friend and I, we would appreciate you putting us up at your house. We are tired of sleeping in animal stables or in some rundown inn."

Lo turned to Gamal and explained everything that had happened and all that was said. Gamal looked rather suspiciously at Almed and questioned whether it was safe to go to the man's house after he accused them of being spies. Gamal said, "I don't trust the man after that. He could be real trouble for us."

Lo responded, "I think he was a little suspicious of us as well and just wanted to see our reaction. After he saw my reaction, he found that what he said was a bit too extreme and unwise and generously apologized. I believe he is truly trying to make amends. I think it will be all right. I believe the man is trustworthy."

With that, Lo turned to Almed and said, "Lead the way. We kindly accept your invitation." Almed took a deep breath and smiled. He clapped both men on the shoulders and said, "Follow me."

After about fifteen minutes through several winding side streets, they arrived at a home with a twelve-foot wall around it. There was a large open gate and inside the gate was a courtyard with two large fig trees on either side of a stone paved walkway. The walkway led to a set of two large double doors made with thick timbers, iron cladding, and large iron hinges. The house was two stories with a three-story wing on the back side of a spacious middle courtyard. It wastruly exceptional. It was clean and well-kept and had a fountain in the center courtyard with four fig trees surrounding the fountain.

Almed, like a kid showing off a new toy, said, "Welcome to my house. You may each have a room to stay in and have a noon meal with me in an hour."

"Truly impressive, a truly impressive home indeed," Lo said admiringly. "What a blessed man you are. I hope we will be able to help you continue that blessed life. Where is a place where we may take care of our donkey? I'm sure the poor animal is worn out and hungry."

Almed laughed and said, "I'm sure he is. Here, let my servant take him and put him in the small barn at the back of the house."

After Lo explained what Almed said, Gamal shook his head and smiled. "Tell him that this is more than just a donkey. This is my mistress's favorite donkey and is a very special animal to her. He is a very special donkey that helped save her son's life. If he doesn't mind, I would like to take the donkey to the barn if his servant could show me the way."

Almed responded with a smile, "Truly, your mistress must be a special lady for all the care you give to even a simple animal as her donkey. You must tell me the tale of her son's life being saved." Almed leaned back, clapped his hands, pointed to his servant, and said, "So be it, we will save that for a future time. My servant will show you the way."

Lo, beaming with pride in his voice, said, "Yes, her name is Marta, and she is a very special person indeed. She is wise and courageous. I have never known of such a prudent and wise person as my mistress. Yes, a very special person indeed."

Gamal left following Almed's servant with the donkey in tow. They went around the house to a small wooden barn at the back of the house. There were two other donkeys there and a small corral for them to wander around in. There was plenty of hay for food. Gamal unloaded the pack frame from the animal and using a handful of straw brushed him down. When Gamal returned from bedding the donkey down, he was just in time for the noon meal. Almed's servants went out of their way to prepare and serve a delicious feast that included a variety of meats, fruits, breads, and cheeses all nicely presented. Almed waved to Gamal to sit next to him, Gamal was hungry and eagerly complied. They had not enjoyed home-prepared food in such a long time that they thoroughly savored every bite.

During the meal, Lo and Almed talked at length about the unique business opportunity that was before them. Lastly at the end of the meal, while they were drinking a mix of wine, water, and fragrant spices that was a common beverage in Philistia, Almed stopped speaking and looked down for about for a short while. The silence made Lo and Gamal a bit uncomfortable. Lo signaled Gamal to just stay silent for now. They remained quiet and enjoyed their drink until Almed finally spoke with a loud voice and said, "I have a plan that I believe will be of great benefit to all of us. Your mistress and her father and their entire household could stay here at my house. Of course, I would charge them a small amount to cover the cost of food and other household items that would be needed, but only enough to cover those costs. Lo, you can watch the books to make sure everything is fair and above board. Your mistress's father and I can go into business immediately, importing cotton and linen and selling it to weavers and merchants throughout all this part of the region. I would have to be a silent partner due to the king's animosity toward me, though I believe that animosity will disappear after a couple of years of well documented taxes paid. Her father and I together could make a market dependent on us for their materials. Who knows, we might even get very rich at this little enterprise of ours. What do you think?"

Lo smiled; it was what they had been discussing for the last two hours. He knew Almed was in desperate financial straits and because of his pride, he needed to feel that this was his idea. In order to not insult the man, he smiled enthusiastically and responded, "Yes, that is an excellent idea. It was what I was trying to put into words, but I was doing a very poor job of getting it across. Yes, it is an excellent idea, and I beg your permission to leave early tomorrow morning and relay your proposal to my mistress. Yes, an excellent idea indeed."

Almed leaned back, "Yes, that would be very good. Go tomorrow and you can even take one of my servants with you. He might be of some assistance when it comes to getting back to Shunem and returning here. He is an Israelite and speaks the Hebrew language, the language of the Philistines and speaks Egyptian as well. He has been of great value in many situations. He is my right hand in business."

Almed called one of his servants into the room and instructed him to pack food for the three of them and told him that he would accompany the Shunammite men back to their home. Lo looked over at the servant and saw that he looked nervous about the prospect of going to Shunem with them. Lo thought about it and decided it was a good idea and understood the man's reluctance. Lo smiled at the servant and said to Almed, "Agreed. I will look after him like he was my own brother." With the last comment, the man's servant looked a little more at ease. Lo explained all that was said to Gamal who was more than just a little happy about the idea of going back home.

Gamal excitedly said, "So we leave tomorrow for sure? You're not kidding me?"

Lo laughed. "No, I'm not kidding you. We are going back home early tomorrow morning."

Gamal clapped his hands and said, "Great! I'm going to check on the donkey, and then I'm going to eat the evening meal and go to sleep early. I have had enough adventure for a while."

Lo had a serious look come across his face and said, "I'm afraid this is just the start of our adventures. There will be plenty of danger, trials, and tragedy ahead. Remember we are talking about seven years and a lot can and will happen in seven years."

Gamal's smile dimmed then brightened again and he said, "All the same we get to go home tomorrow. I'll take that for now." He then walked off, singing to himself. Lo just shook his head and laughed.

*****

The next morning the rooster crowed long after the two Shunammite men had eaten, packed their animal, and set out for home with Almed's servant. It was another hour before the sun would break the horizon. By the time the sun was all the way up, they were a couple of miles out of town and feeling a sense of relief to be heading home. Both men felt uncomfortable the whole time they were in Ashkelon. Lo felt even more uneasy whenever one of their priests even looked in their general direction. An anxious premonition overtook him as he pondered the possibility that before this was all over, they could have a serious confrontation with these priests.

The road back home was long and dreaded. Each mile felt like an eternity. After five days of hard travel, they finally were out of Philistia. They both stopped and took a deep breath and looked back, both glad to be out of Philistia territory. Almed's servant understood how they felt; he hadn't seen his home since he was twelve. "Oh, how I don't want to go back there," said Gamal, looking back down the road they just traveled. "I have never felt so anxious in my life.

Not even Saana made me feel as unsettled as I have the pastcouple of weeks. I really don't like that place. Are you sure there is no other way?"

"It's not for me to decide," Lo lamented. He also felt uncomfortable about returning to Philistia, but Gamal's constant complaining and worrying over the last two days was getting on his nerves. Lo started walking again and said, "This is the prophet's idea and has all the support of our mistress and her father. I know it looks risky, but basically, it is our only viable option. Especially since we found Almed in Ashkelon and all the opportunity that presents. So shake off that complaining attitude of yours and make up your mind we are returning to Ashkelon, probably within the week. Now, let's go home."

Just as they were crossing the border from Philistia, Gamal saw some sinister-looking men on a hillside watching them. He pointed them out to his two companions, and the three men picked up their pace considerably. "I don't know who they are, but I don't like the look of them," said Almed's servant. "I truly believe they are bandits looking for easy prey."

With that, they each found a branch by the roadside that they could use as a club and kept a close watch for the men on the hillside to try and stop them, which never happened.

Gamal observed, "I believe we will see those men again. We better be ready if we do."

13

A New Adventure

A level of anxiety crept up on Marta as she watched Lo and Gamal disappear into the distance. She loved the two men like they were her brothers. They experienced so much together over the years. She was sure that the death of Saana would cause their life to be so much better, but here they were looking at another major challenge. She lamented out loud, "Will the miseries ever end? Will they ever end?"

Akeem noticed a quiet but deeply worried look on his daughter's face and saw the tears welling up in her eyes. He put his hand on her shoulder and said, "They will be all right. They are both smart and resourceful. They will be just fine." He patted her shoulder. Her father had changed so much since her sixteenth birthday.

Marta turned to Ishaman, her head field servant, and in her authoritative voice, she said, "Now, let's talk about the livestock. What plans did you and Gamal come up with for the livestock? It sounds like things are going to get desperate, so I need to know where we are at with our short-term and longterm planning."

He responded in a patronizing manner, "We have it all under control, no need for you to worry."

Her father suppressed a laugh and thought, *He still has absolutely no idea who he is dealing with.*

Marta smiled and walked up to the man's face within two feet and, in a low voice, said, "I asked you a question or, more importantly, addressed the question to my senior field hand—that is, if he still wants to be the senior field hand. Well, do you?" She locked her eyes on his and didn't blink. He was shaken.

He was used to being in charge, and except for Saana, no one dared challenge him. He knew she meant business and wouldn't think twice about demoting him if he crossed her. He timidly responded, "Yes, mistress, I do want to keep my position. I apologize for my insolence. Follow me to the large barn. I will show what we have planned."

They disappeared into the barn with Marta's father and Eli following close behind. It was pleasing to Eli to see his mother put Ishaman in his place. So many times, the man had given him a hard time when he went out to the fields to help in any way he could. Eli would say to himself, "Someday I will be in charge and will replace that man and send him packing." The thought made him smile.

Hadiza called to her two daughters and led them back into house. "We have a lot of work to do to get ready for an extended trip. Pick out what you want to take with you, but remember, we will be very limited on what we can bring. Just the necessities. Oh, and incidentally, I will be going over what you pick out." The girls were smiling until their mother's final statement then they both headed into the house with heads dropped.

After Ishaman finished briefing Marta and her father, they all went into the house for food, drink, and some more planning. It had been a stressful morning. Ishaman was surprised when Marta invited him to join them. He still had not figured her out completely, but he was beginning to. Not that it really mattered in the long run, he had some plans of his own. He said to himself, "Never again will I underestimate her. It's a lesson I won't soon forget." While going over their plans, they determined that they were going to give Lo and Gamal five weeks, and if they didn't return by then, her father would go looking for them.

Akeem went back to his house to let his family and servants know what they had organized. They were both excited and fearful at same time. His family had never been out of Shunem in their lives; they didn't know what to expect, and the fear of the unknown was very difficult to conquer. Marta's mother asked, "Is the prophet coming with us?"

Akeem shook his head and said, "No, he isn't. He has given us advice, but as far as I know, he is not coming with us. Philistia is much greener than this region. The people there are much like us, but their religion and some of their customs are very different. I'm not real comfortable when their priests are around, but I have been in the region several times, and I am not too worried about the people. There will be a group of us so if we keep close together. I think we will be safe."

Marta's father briefed her brothers and went to a few of his friends and told them what the prophet had warned him about. He emphasized the famine would be very severe and would last seven years, but none of them were moved. All refused to join them. He went to his neighbors, but they were insistent, "I'm not leaving my land and home for robbers to steal everything I own," said one. Others were not about to go to Philistia for any reason. They had been enemies for hundreds of years, and they were afraid that the Philistines would abuse them, take their families, and rob them of whatever they had left. No matter what her father said, his friends thought Akeem was crazy for even considering a move to Philistia. Exasperated, he went back to his house fuming and muttering about how foolish his friends were being.

Marta's brothers, on the other hand, were glad to be forewarned and even happier that there was a plan that included them staying in Shunem. They both had several children and were very apprehensive about traveling to Ashkelon with the young. With the twelve-foot-high wall and the large iron reinforced gate, they felt that they would be safe behind it. They also considered the strength of family and the fifteen male servants that they had between them would be enough manpower to drive off any pillagers.

When he got back to his home, Akeem saw the house was bustling. The servants were sorting their belongings, his wife was running about shouting orders. It was organized chaos. He smiled and went to his wife and put his hand on her shoulder and said, "We aren't going anywhere for weeks. Why are you hurrying so? There is plenty of time. If you hurry too much, things will get missed. Now let's sit down and figure all this out. You, me, our family, and the servants. We need a plan before we start doing anything." He was the consummate businessman, which is why he was successful, and with the help of Saana, he was now one of the richest men in Shunem. His sons came to the house about an hour later, and he went over the plans to make the property as secure as possible and decide how to set up a defense for his house.

Marta was also every bit the organizer, but this was new to her, and she was not sure where to start or even finish for that matter. She sat down with Hadiza and started to plan their trip and long stay in a foreign land that neither of them had been to. Except for her trip to Mt. Carmel, she had never been more than a mile out of Shunem. She called everyone together in the courtyard and said, "Okay, let's prioritize a list of things we will need to take with us. We must be careful to not over or underpack items. There's always a possibility of sending someone back for additional things we might need, so overpacking is our biggest issue we need to avoid. Food and money are a must, but then, we will also need blankets, oil for lamps, grain for the animals, and so many other things. We need to assess what wagons and livestock we will need to transport all these things to be able to live there. We don't want to start packing things and then unpack to go through all of it again to figure out what we are taking. So have your daughters stop packing and start getting lunch ready while you and I work this out."

Hadiza saw the logic in her mistress's approach and did as she asked. When she came to her daughters, they were arguing and shouting at one another about what the other should and should not take. With a loud command from their mother, "Girls, get the midday meal ready now!" both dropped what they were doing and immediately ran to the kitchen. When their mother used that tone of voice, they didn't argue, they obeyed immediately. There was never room for argument with their mother when she used that tone of voice.

*****

The next two weeks were a series of planning, packing, unpacking, and repacking. They revisited their plans over and over again. Deciding what to pack was far more difficult than they all dreamed it would be. At their first attempt Marta's father, who had traveled quite a bit and was used to long trips, looked at what they packed and said, "You and your mother are just alike. You will need twenty wagons to take all this! You will have four wagons, ten mules, ten donkeys, and eight oxen. That is going to limit how much you can take. And as far as coming back here to get any additional items, that's out of the question. When the famine starts, that dangerous road will become much more dangerous. Desperate people will be around every curve. People who are normally decent will become vicious. Your friends will change into savages. I have seen famine in other lands and what it does to people is horrible. Desperate people do terrible things to live. They just want to live, even if means robbing their closest friend or even killing someone, even killing a relative and eating them. It's horrible what desperate people will do. We won't be coming back here to get anything. One or two servants with a couple of donkeys may come by stealth and check on things and bring some food on the back of the donkeys, but no wagons. By then, you wouldn't get two miles with wagons in tow."

Mother and daughter were shocked by what Akeem said. Both ladies looked at what they had set out for packing and tried to think of anything that they didn't need; they couldn't. Marta's father said loudly, "Ladies, there is a vast amount of goods here you can live without. Take two changes of clothing. Take enough bedding for one bed apiece, you don't need ten blankets each. We will buy wine there, so we don't need five vats of wine. You'd kill the poor mules by trying to pull it all the way to Ashkelon. Honestly, ladies, you are not even trying to limit your packing. It's not taking your house with you. It's taking enough to start a house there. Just to start a house—not move a house. Only bring the bare minimum to start a life there. We will find what we need when we get there. Their cities are much larger than Shunem, so don't worry, we will be able to find the provisions we need when we get there. Four wagons—four wagons for each family are all you will get. Make the most of them."

One evening four weeks later, three very tired men and a donkey walked up to Marta's house and knocked on the door. Seeta came and opened the door, and when she saw the men, she screamed so loud that everyone in the house came running to see what was wrong. They were all extremely happy to see Lo and Gamal return safely and wondered who the stranger was with them. Lo introduced

Almed's Hebrew servant to everyone and explained what he was there for. They were so excited to hear that they found a house they could all live in, and that there was someone there waiting to receive them. Marta was extremely glad to know that they didn't have to start from scratch, though she was a little concerned about living in a house with another family. Some small concerns continued; however, the fear of the unknown had greatly diminished and faded from tormenting to more of a nagging worry.

Marta hurried Lamel to run to her father's house and let him and her mother know about the men returning. Her father dashed out the door and came to Marta's house out of breath and excited to find out any news. When Lo explained what happened on their adventure to Ashkelon and how they met, of all things, a linen and cotton merchant. He told him that the man had an empty warehouse that they could use and how he had invited them to stay at his house while they were in Philistia. Sat it was a very large house and would accommodate the whole group. Lo also told the father about the man's tax situation and how it was ruining his business and the strong possibility of a partnership that would benefit them both. Marta's father's smile got bigger with every sentence. It was better than he could have ever hoped for. He went to his own house to finish up packing the mules and wagons. The packing and planning took another five days, but finally, it was all done.

The afternoon before their departure, Michael came running to the courtyard where Marta and Hadiza were and shouted, "I saw him! I saw him! The prophet on the way down the road." The whole household ran to the road. Elisha and Gehazi were about one hundred yards from the house, and they waved as soon as they saw Marta, Eli, and her servants. Elisha greeted them in the Shunammite language, which excited all of them. It was the first time he had ever spoken to any of them directly in their own language. It was a little thing that meant so much. With Gehazi translating, the prophet said, "I see you are just about ready to travel. Where are you going again?"

Elisha smiled and took in a deep breath and said, "My God is with you. Don't be so concerned about how you will fair when you get there, He has prepared the way. You will prosper." He looked at them with a seriousness that they could all feel, and he repeated with a firmer tone, "I promise, you will prosper. Now I must go and be about the work of my God. There is a king who needs to be reminded how he got to be king. I just wanted to see how you were fairing and encourage you that God is with you." With that, he turned and motioned to Gehazi to move on. They were around a bend and out of sight in just a few minutes.

They all worked hard loading the wagons and getting the animals ready. At the end of the day, Marta stretched out and groaned, "Well, we are set to go. If you think of anything else you need to bring"—she smiled—"I'm sorry, but you'll need to leave it. We don't have room for anything else. Now let's go to bed and be up at the first rooster crow." The group walked slowly back to the house and were in bed and asleep within minutes.

14
Off to Ashkelon

The rooster crowed long before daylight, and the whole group was slow to get up but with some encouragement from Marta in her house and her father in his house, they managed to beat the sunrise. Everyone was sore and stiff from packing and loading but excited at the same time. The words of the prophet motivated them so that they were now actually looking forward to the adventure. The mules were stubborn and the worst to get started—it seemed that they were determined to set the morning into chaos. But by first light, they were on the road and rolling along smoothly. Before long, Shunem was out of sight, and now reality was setting in.

Akeem's head looked as if it were on a swivel, Marta perceived her father was very nervous. The look of concern on his face had Marta and the rest of the group nervous. Lo tried to comfort everyone by stating, "Relax, Gamal and I traveled this road a few days ago and didn't have any problems at all, we'll be just fine." He had mentioned the men on the hillside to Marta's father but didn't mention it to any of the others. Akeem was not surprised that there were what appeared to be bandits near the road, watching for the unsuspecting and unprepared. Akeem turned to Lo and was visibly angry. "You didn't have baggage, livestock, and women with you. So be vigilant, I believe this is going to get serious real soon. I feel it in my bones. There is one good thing, though, the fact that we have several men in the group that may intimidate bandits enough to keep them away. I suggest each of you carry a staff with you, both men and women, so you'll look even more intimidating. Remember the men you saw coming back to Shunem Gamal."

"Men? What men?" Marta said with surprise. "What men are you talking about?"

Gamal responded, "We didn't want to worry you, but on our way back, we saw some men on a hillside and thought they might be following us. Nothing came of it, but they did have us a little worried at first."

Marta was furious. "Don't ever assume to protect me by holding back information! Don't ever do that again! Do you understand?" Both Lo and Gamal and even her father nodded, being a bit embarrassed.

Marta shouted out an order. "Everyone find something to use as a weapon. A branch or a handy farm tool but something you can use to protect yourself and walk with it in full display so people can see them. Then maybe any bandits will think twice about bothering us." Each man and woman picked a branch from the trees next to the stream that ran by the road and fashioned it into a walking staff. Of course Eli picked one that was far too large for his stature and was having a difficult time handling it. His grandfather just smiled and congratulated Eli on his selection. "That looks like a good weapon. Maybe they will think twice about taking you on."

Eli walked proudly, holding his big stick with both hands. Michael, Marta, and Misam each grabbed a limb for themselves, though smaller than the others, they kept them on full display trying to look tough.

Marta's father warned that the first day would be tiring, and each successive day would be more and more exhausting. It was a warning that proved right. By day 5 on the road, they were physically exhausted. Carrying baggage, chasing livestock, watching out for bandits, and especially the sleepless nights keeping watch was taking its toll on them. Akeem advised that they should find a wide place by the road to rest for a day. They found a place near a small stream that crossed the road, and there they camped and refreshed themselves. When they started out again, they gained some needed strength but were by no means "rested."

Later that day, they saw six men on the hillsides who appeared to be following them and watching their every move. Marta's father set a watch schedule that night, but no one bothered them until the next day. When they rounded a bend, there were two men standing in the middle of the road with clubs in their hands. One shouted out in the Philistine language with his hand raised, apparently telling the group to stop. Akeem shouted out to the group, "Don't stop, just keep going. Gamal, Lamel, Lo, come up front with me." He motioned to two of his male servants and to Misam to come up front as well. Then he instructed two other male servants to look after the livestock along with the four that were already there. He had his wife go to the center of the group for her protection. Marta and the other women lined up behind her father and the other men in front. All the women carried their staffs and tried to look as menacing as possible. Eleven-year-old Eli, looking a bit ridiculous with his oversized staff, stood next to his mother to "protect her."

The larger of the two men in the road shouted louder for them to stop, but the group just kept walking right toward him. The man and his companion started to look nervous and glanced to the side at the other men on the hillside. Akeem could see four other men on a hillside that looked equally as rough and were also armed with clubs. Again, Akeem shouted out, "Just keep going. They are fewer than us, and I can tell they are not so sure of their ability to intimidate us. That's what they hope to do, intimidate us so we won't put up a fight. Keep walking no matter what. If they come down to the road, I need all the other men that are with the livestock to come up here with us. Make sure you are carrying your staff so they can see it. I can tell that they are already thinking twice about what to do next."

The man that was shouting, comparably larger and more muscular than his companions, saw that Marta's father was doing all the talking in the group and perceived he was the leader and ran up to him with a club in hand only to be met with a vicious smack in the side with Gamal's staff. That stopped the man in his tracks. With the wind knocked out of him, the man dropped to his knees, trying to take a breath and was met with another blow to the head from Akeem's staff. The man lay moaning on the ground. Marta's father signaled to the man's companion to pick up his friend and get him out of the way or suffer the same fate. The men on the hillside backed up and started walking over the top of the hill until they were out of sight. The group all started to shout and celebrate. Marta felt relief when she saw the other men retreat over the hilltop.

Akeem was not so relieved. "They aren't going away as you think. They are going to follow us on the road until dark and then try something. Believe me, they haven't gone very far. But now, the leader has a score to settle with me, and he is not going to stop until we stop him, and that's just what I intend to do. Gamal, you round up all the male servants and meet me here in a half an hour. Make sure they are armed with at least one staff or any sharp farming implement they can use as a weapon. Marta, have your female servants arm themselves with their staffs and watch the livestock. Pull the wagons into a square and put the animals inside the square. That can offer some defense against anyone who tries to get at either you or the livestock."

Marta was shocked at her father. She knew he was tough, but the way he and Gamal handled the head bandit flabbergasted her. She was impressed by the way he had marshalled everyone into a real fighting force. For the first time, she realized her father was a man to be reckoned with when pushed, can be brutal can be brutal if needed. In a little less than half an hour, the men were assembled, and the women were herding the animals into the square they created with the wagons. Four of the men had scythes, three had wooden pitchforks and the rest had staffs. They were ready for whatever the father had in mind. Akeem stood on one of the wagons and said, "Men, those bandits will go to get reinforcements and will be waiting for us to make a mistake and catch us off guard. If we don't do something first and quickly, they will eventually catch us making that mistake that could end up being fatal. So we are not waiting for them to come to us, we are going out to them. We are going to catch them off guard instead, before they can call on their friends. We are going to do the very thing they don't expect, a surprise ambush! Whether we take the battle to them, or they come for us, the fight is inevitable. So let's get our blows in first."

The men were excited and nervous at the same time, but they knew Akeem was right. Lo, probably the weakest of them, said, "They started it, now let's finish it." With that, the men set out. Akeem had two men come with him while the rest stayed about a hundred yards back. When the three got to the top of a hill next to the road, they saw the bandits sitting around a camp re in a group, eating and talking. Akeem went back to the rest of the men and sent four around the left side of the hill and four around the right side of the hill while he and the remaining five men, headed straight for the bandits. As far as they could see, there were six bandits altogether. The leader was the largest, and they all looked like tough characters.

When the bandits saw the six Shunammite men coming toward them, they were surprised. They stopped talking, stood up, and grabbed whatever they were using for a weapon. The leader started walking toward Akeem and stopped about ten feet short of him. The two groups just stood there, trying to stare each other down. The bandits started getting restless and started acting as if they were going to attack when the other two groups of Shunammite men came from both sides. The bandits realized they were both outmaneuvered and outnumbered. They started to look for an avenue of escape, but Akeem had anticipated this and signaled the men to get behind them and close off any avenue of escape. He also let the bandits know no mercy would be given. Then Lo let out a scream that startled the bandits and ignited the Shunammite men to charge. The battle lasted about five minutes, and when it was over, three of the bandits were dead, and the remaining three were wounded and were no longer a threat. Only three of the Shunammite men were injured, and only one was seriously injured—Lo.

With the skirmish over, Akeem rounded up the men and ordered them return to the wagons. Four carried Lo on a hastily made stretcher made with two staffs and a blanket from the bandit's camp. When Marta saw the men coming back, she was relieved—that is, until she saw Lo on a stretcher with a broken left leg and two large cuts on his left arm and shoulder. She immediately had them make room on one of the wagons and started to tend to his wounds. Gamal and Marta's mother showed Marta how to tend the broken leg, and Lo talked her through how to treat and bandage the two cuts. It took about an hour to bind up his injuries.

Akeem spoke up and said, "These men probably have friends, so we must not stay here. We have to start moving within the hour. We do not want to be in this place come dark. If they do have friends, they will probably outnumber us. So, everyone, quickly prepare yourselves to be on the move now!" The idea of the bandit's friends coming for revenge was enough to stir everyone to be ready in haste. They had to leave a few things behind to make room for Lo in the wagon, but they counted those things as little value in their situation.

As they rounded a curve and out of the area, Marta felt a huge sense of relief. The idea of running into those people in the middle of the night frightened her, though she would never show it. It was well after sundown before they stopped. The animals were spent and so were all of them, and especially Lo who was in considerable pain. With each bump in the road, he thought someone had hit him in the leg with a hammer. Being able to stop was a godsend to him.

"How are you doing?" Marta asked Lo. "Is there anything more we can do for you?"

Lo looked at her with a weak smile. "Just get us to Ashkelon, and I will be happy."

In four more nerve-wracking days, looking over their shoulder for more bandits, they were on a hill overlooking Ashkelon, and it appeared to them to be one of the most beautiful sights in the world. They were weary, exhausted, and yearned for the safety of being in a house with a high wall around it.

"Oh, to feel safe again," Marta muttered. Her mother was standing beside her and patted Marta on the shoulder.

Gamal and Almed's servant went ahead to announce their arrival while Akeem encouraged everyone to keep their current pace and not give in to trying to get there faster. He stood in front of everyone and said, "When you hurry livestock, too many things can go wrong. Just go at the same pace as we have been. We will get there soon enough. I understand everyone is tired and just want to get there and feel safe, but haste only increases the chance of making mistakes." Marta voiced her agreement and suggested to her father that the two of them go to the front of the group and set the pace. Gamal came back and met the group to show them the way. The group arrived at Almed's house late in the late afternoon, and Almed was at the gate to greet them along with his servants. They had prepared a feast for everyone to celebrate their arrival, and by it, he had nearly used up the last of his food reserves.

"Welcome to my home," Almed said in Egyptian.

Akeem responded, "We thank you for your hospitality and are deeply indebted to you for your generosity. This group is pretty much exhausted and are looking forward to some food and rest."

Almed replied, "I have been looking forward to meeting you and the lady that I have heard so much about and has so inspired her servants that they were willing to come here at great risk to find a safe place for her and her family."

Akeem stepped forward and pointed to Marta and said, "Sir, let me introduce the lady. She is indeed everything we boasted about. She is the mistress of a large house, a friend to her servants, and a legend to her family."

Lo interpreted what was said, and Marta blushed at the introduction. She smiled and bowed to Almed, saying through Lo, "My father sometimes exaggerates. I am just a humble woman, and I am willing to help you and my father in any way I can. Yes, my servants are my friends, and I love each one of them as family, and I think they feel the same about me. My father is my inspiration. We would have never made it here if it had not been for his leadership."

Akeem introduced himself; and immediately, he and Almed started talking about business, ignoring the rest of the group and walking into the house.

Marta turned to one of Almed's servants and using her hands and gestures asked, "Where can we put the livestock and bring the wagons?" Then she said to their servants, "Once we have the livestock temporarily corralled and fed, we will go into the house and eat and rest. We will unload the wagons in the morning. Hadiza, you and your daughters unload some food from the wagons and bring it into the house." Again, she used gestures to ask Almed's servants about helping unload the provisions from the wagons. They understood instantly and were more than a little excited to help. They knew they had just about used up all their food and were becoming concerned that one of them would be sold off to be able to feed the others. Seeing the amount of food Marta's group brought was a tremendous relief and a joy. They enjoyed a bountiful meal that night and were in bed just shortly after sunset.

Almed was relieved at their presence; he was starting to get really concerned about what he was going to do for food enough for all of them until he heard how much the Shunammites had brought. He slept better that night than he had in many months. He was beginning to think that the arrival of the two Shunammite men was just a dream, and he was going to wake up to a terrible reality.

The next morning, the whole household was up with the sun. They settled the livestock in their permanent pens and then proceeded to unload the wagons. The house was large, but still, the women servants had to share two rooms and the male servants had four rooms between them. Marta had the largest room, and her mother and father picked a room next door to her. Though their room was a bit smaller than they were used to, they wanted to be next to their daughter and passed up a larger room on the other side of the house. It only took a couple of hours to unpack and settle in. There was a cheerful mood throughout the house. Everyone had a place in the house that was comfortable. A high wall around the house made them feel safe, and Almed did all that he could to make them feel at home.

15
Business and Taxes

In a few months, Almed and Akeem had the linen and cotton import business up, running, and at full speed. They soon learned that they shared some of the same business contacts, which made it even more helpful to expedite the business. With their contacts and knowledge of the industry, they rapidly became prosperous. Their success got the attention of the king who held a healthy distrust of Almed. Learning of the king's interest in their business from some business contacts and knowing the history of his distrust in Ahmed, Akeem requested an audience with the king, and it was granted. One of Almed's servants accompanied him as an interpreter. Akeem was learning the language but was still far from fluent.

When they arrived at the king's palace, they were met on the front steps by the tax collector who had created so many problems for Almed. The tax collector demanded, "What do you want from the king?"

Akeem looked him straight in the eye and replied, "That's between the king and me, so move aside, or do you want me to report to the king that the business deal I have for him was intercepted by one of his underlings? I have no business with you and do not intend to any time soon. Now get out of my way. The king is waiting for me."

The tax collector stepped aside for this obviously tough foreigner. He was used to intimidating others, and it was seldom intimidated by anyone other than the king himself or his advisors, but this man caught him off guard and left him feeling like a teenager caught in the act of some prank. He was not sure what this man and the king had talked about already, so he decided to wait as see what would happen before he tried to somehow intervene.

Akeem stepped into the courtyard where the king was sitting in a large ornamental chair, receiving visitors and petitioners. There were two guards on either side of him and several advisors to his left. Ashkelon was a large city and wielded considerable financial and military power in the region, so this king had some real clout in the region when it came to business issues. He was about the same height as Akeem and a bit overweight. Ultimately, he had the power of life and death but was a very pragmatic man. He appeared to be a no nonsense type of individual, and upon Akeem's entry, the king locked eyes on him. Akeem didn't avert the king's gaze but, contrary to custom, stared back directly into the king's eyes. He wanted to show that he was not intimidated but was there as a potential business partner. Right or wrong, he was in this all the way. The king immediately motioned him to come closer and said, "Who is this with you, foreigner?"

Almed's servant interpreted and then responded that he was there to interpret for the Shunammite. "Although he can speak some of our language, he wanted to make sure that he didn't insult the king with his poor language skills." Then through the interpreter, Akeem started to explain his plan for the king and himself to corner the linen market in the region. That there was a way to increase the kings tax revenue through not only importing linen and cotton but also in making linen and cotton cloth to sell in several cities in the region. The king leaned forward and only had a few questions, but the biggest question was "Who would oversee this venture? Are you the only one I will deal with?"

This is was where Akeem was a little nervous. "Almed the Egyptian and myself. We are the linen merchants with the most experience in Ashkelon. My family has been in the linen and cotton business for generations. I have contacts from Egypt all the way to the kingdom of Kush where most of our cotton comes from, and I have contacts all the way to Damascus."

Seeing the skeptical look on the king's face, Akeem pressed on and became very straightforward about the plans. "I have been in business with Almed for several months, and I am even living in his house. The stories I hear about him not paying his taxes doesn't align with the man I have come to know." Now the father started to press into a dangerous area of discussion. "Out of curiosity, sir, I looked and noticed Almed's receipts, and I discovered that his taxes were indeed paid and on time. Then I asked myself who would benefit the most from informing the king that Almed was not paying his taxes?"

The king sat back with a serious look as Akeem continued. "But who would say that they were not paid and why would they say that? Consider this, did Almed's tax records ever show that he was late before this? Were not his taxes significant?"

The king rolled his head back in deep thought. Akeem recognized that he had the king's curiosity then continued, "Who confiscated all of Almed's goods, and how much did he take? Do you know for sure? Did you have someone from your court observe the collection? According to Almed's purchase receipts, the total amount of confiscated items didn't match his records that said what he actually had on hand." The king slowly shook his head and now was leaning forward.

Seeing that he had the king's full interest, Akeem risked it all by continuing, "Did you know that over fifty bolts of linen and ten large bales of cotton were confiscated? I wonder how many were reported to you compared to what was actually taken? If the king checked the tax collector's records, I believe he will find a significant discrepancy."

The king replied, "You bring up some interesting information and suggestions. We will check and see what the tax collector has to say. But you know you have stepped into some dangerous ground here. You know the penalty for falsely accusing a representative of the king is immediate death."

Akeem nodded that he did understand the risk. The king looked him in the eye, and Akeem did not avert his gaze one bit. The king grunted, turned to one of his advisors, and commanded that the tax collector be summoned with his tax records in hand. The king ordered a chair be brough for Marta's father to sit on and that they would wait for the tax collector to arrive. He was impressed with the man's courage and confidence.

It took about an hour for the tax collector to come rather breathlessly into the courtyard. He had two servants with him, each carrying several large books. The king motioned the tax collector to come forward, and that's when the tax collector saw Akeem. His face immediately turned from smiling and deferential to a frown and a quizzical look. He stammered, "Wha-wha-what may I do for my king?"

The king replied, "Look in your books and tell me how many and what type of items you confiscated from Almed the linen merchant about two years ago. More specifically, how many bolts of linen and bales of cotton you confiscated."

The tax collector looked at Akeem who was smiling and realized that he was trapped. If he said the wrong amount, he would be found out in the books. His only option was to make up a contrived story of a recent discovery of an error in the books. The tax collector said weakly, "Sire, I was just going to come to you about a recent error found in the books. Let me see here." He took one of the books and opened it up and turned several pages. "Oh yes, here it is. We under counted the bolts of linen and bales of cotton. Some of the linen and bales of cotton were outside of the warehouse and weren't included in the count. Hmm, let me see…that would be thirty bolts of linen and eight bales of cotton. Yes, we undercounted by twenty bolts of linen and two bales of cotton. My apologies, sire. We will get the value of those bales in gold to you immediately."

The king looked at him and smiled, "Twenty bolts of very expensive linen and two bales of cotton left out in the weather? How very careless of the linen merchant, wouldn't you agree? What do you think, Mr. Linen Merchant? Wouldn't that be extremely unusual for an experienced linen merchant with room in a warehouse to leave linen and cotton outside in the weather and where thieves could just walk away with these very expensive items?"

Marta's father replied, "Yes, sire, that would be highly unlikely. As a matter of fact, almost unbelievably negligent. What would be even more unbelievable is if it were more like fifty bolts of linen and ten bales instead of the few that were reported. But I guess mistakes can be made even by the most experienced of people. Wouldn't you agree, sire?"

The king looked the tax collector in the eyes and said, "Yes, I would agree. Mistakes can be made even by the best of us. How about you, tax collector, wouldn't you agree?"

The tax collector smiled a nervous smile and said, "Definitely. I have been doing this a long time, and here it is. I made a mistake, but I will make it right immediately. If the king would give me a day or so to get the money together."

The king turned to his guard and commanded, "Take this tax collector and throw him in prison." To the captain of the guard, he ordered, "Bring me the king's treasurer and have him go over the tax collector's books and report back to me what he finds tomorrow at this time." He turned to Akeem and said, "Come back to me this time tomorrow, and we will discuss this matter further. Oh, and bring Almed the linen merchant with you."

Akeem left and headed directly back to the warehouse to tell Almed everything that had happened.

"What do you think he will find in the books?" Almed asked. He was still a little nervous, especially about going back with Akeem the next day into the presence of an angry king. Sings could go bad very quickly as he had already found out once before.

Akeem tried to comfort Almed by stating, "By the reaction of the tax collector, who looked like a little boy caught in the act, I think the king will find a considerable amount of cheating done by the illustrious official. By this time tomorrow, I believe we will be rich men." Marta's father leaned back on a bale of cotton with a large mischievous grin on his face.

Almed put his hand on Akeem's shoulder and said, "Either very rich men or very dead men. You know you took a tremendous risk in doing this. This king is responsible for the death of a great many people. Yes, there is a lot of risk involved here."

Marta was listening and shouted out, "Risk? What risk? What are you talking about? What kind of risk did you take, Father?"

Almed replied, "The risk for falsely reporting a representative of the king is death. This king is very defensive of his representatives and has put to death many men and women in defense of his own. They may have been right, but if the king could not find evidence that confirmed the complaint, and quite honestly, he does not look very hard, you take a very bad risk indeed."

Marta blurted out, "Why would you take such a risk? We need you alive, not another one of the king's victims."

Her father smiled and pointed to Almed. "This man risked quite a lot inviting us into his house, and he deserves our help, no matter what the risk. Now this is the last of this conversation, understand? We will be seeing the king tomorrow. What is done is done."

Marta furiously turned and stomped out of the room.

The next day, Akeem and Almed stood in front of the king. Almed was extremely nervous, but Marta's father was cool, calm, and confident of the outcome. Akeem saw the tax collector off to the side with a guard on either side, and he looked terrified. The king motioned Akeem and Almed to come near and said, "There appears to be a horrible mistake made, right, tax collector?" As the king kept his gaze on the two linen merchants, he continued, "What about hundreds of 'mistakes' a person makes? Hundreds of horrible mistakes? How does a person fix them? It would be difficult, would it not?"

The tax collector was now on his knees shaking violently. "Sire, I don't know what to say. There may have been a few lapses in judgment on my part and areas that I overlooked. I was so busy about the king's business. Please forgive me."

The king turned and looked at the tax collector directly and replied, "Did I give you permission to speak? Let's see now. I believe I will show you the same mercy you showed Almed the linen merchant. All your property is now forfeit. All your servants are now mine. All your money now goes to the treasury, and you are now the servant of Almed the linen merchant. Now I think that is a very fair exchange for your life, don't you?"

The tax collector started to say something and saw the king lean toward him with a deep frown and decided: "Yes, sire" was the wiser of his options. The king sat back and said, "Good, then we agree. Of course, we can always look at the other option. What do you say, Almed?"

Almed locked his gaze on the tax collector and said, "It was a hard decision for me to make. I think he would probably make a mediocre servant at best, but since you offered such a generous gift, I thank the king for his merciful, wise, and noble decision."

The king slapped his hands on his knees and said, "Good, then all there is to do is have my captain of the army oversee the details. Captain, tie the hands of this 'retired' tax collector and escort him through the town announcing his fate and then take him to Almed the linen merchant's house. When you get there, make a public declaration that this man is now Almed's servant and usher him into the house. Post a guard just in case he decides he has changed his mind about the arrangement. If he causes any trouble, bring him back to me. Oh, and, linen merchant, I will make sure you are reimbursed for the things the tax collector took from you."

Then the king turned to Akeem and said, "Now let's talk about this business arrangement you are proposing." They talked until dark. The king invited them to dine with him, and they continued their discussions well into the night. The king agreed to the arrangement with a few adjustments on what his percent of the share would be and had his scribe write out the agreement.

Just before the departure of Almed and Akeem, the king said, "Come back tomorrow and my scribe will have a copy of the agreement for you." With that, the two men went home patting each other on the back and laughing on the turn of events for the tax collector.

16

The Priest

Early the next morning, Lo was at the fish market with Hadiza's daughter Misam, shopping for fresh fish. Lo hadn't done any of the food shopping since arriving in Ashkelon because of his broken leg that was now finally well enough to go out into the city. Hadiza, who normally did the shopping, woke up feeling ill that morning and asked if Lo would escort her daughter to the market. She wanted someone to look out for her daughter's safety. His leg still bothered him, and he had a noticeable limp, but the pain was nearly gone. Hadiza didn't send Lo with her daughter so much for safety's sake, but more of the comfort of his company.

The market's smells were almost overwhelming. Lo hated the smell of fish and was nearly sick when they first walked onto the docks where the market was. Misam thought it was funny to see the great Lo brought to his knees by the smell of a bunch of small fish. Lo didn't see the humor in it at all. As they walked up to the first table of fish, Lo noticed a priest standing just outside the market area watching them intently. It wasn't a casual glance that Lo could just brush off; this was an intent and almost angry stare. He tried to avoid looking back but found himself occasionally glancing at the priest to see if he was still staring. He was. He slowly grabbed Misam's arm and said, "We need to leave here."

Surprised, Misam pulled her arm away and said, "We aren't done yet. I haven't even started to buy the first fish yet."

Lo spoke quietly, "Hold your voice down. We are being watched. See that man in the purple cloak over there? He is a priest of Baal.

151

They are terrible people, and he has been watching us since we got here. Please just follow me and let's go back home for now and shop later."

Misam was perturbed. "He's not watching us. You are letting your imagination run away with you. I told my mother that I would get the fish for supper, and that's just what I intend to do."

Lo noticed that the priest now had two other priests with him and three soldiers. He pointed in their direction and was adamant about something. Lo could not think of what might have triggered his attention, but he perceived it was not good. In a semi-panicked voice, Lo pleaded, "Please, Misam, we need to leave now. This is looking very bad."

Misam looked at the priest again and decided that Lo may be right, "Okay, you could be right. Let's go home. I can always come back a little later." They turned and started to walk away from the market and heard the priest yell. Lo grabbed Misam's arm and screamed, "Run!" They both took off running as fast as they could, but the market was crowded, and Lo's leg had never been the same after it was broken in the battle with the bandits. They seemingly lost sight of the priests and the soldiers, but when they reached the edge of the market, they were intercepted by the three soldiers. Trying to run past them, Lo stumbled and fell. He shouted to Misam, "Run, run for your life! Don't look back, run!"

Misam sprinted through the crowd again as the soldiers stumbled over Lo. The guards lost sight of her, so they grabbed Lo by both arms and held him to the ground until one of the priests arrived. The priest looked down at Lo, smiled, and said, "What have we here? A foreigner? A spy? A heretic? Well, which are you? Perhaps you are all three. I've had my eye on your group for quite a while, and it only makes sense that you are staying with an Egyptian heretic. What goes on in that large house of yours?" He leaned forward close to Lo's face and said in a whisper, "We will find out, yes, we will find out." The priest tied Lo's hands in front of him and pulling him along motioned to the soldiers to follow.

Misam ran as fast as she could to Almed's house. She banged on the gate as loud as she could and screamed "Help, please help Lo!" Several servants came running to the gate and let her in.

Marta came running from in the house and shouted, "What do you mean 'help Lo'? What has happened to Lo? Where is he?" Marta grabbed Misam's shoulders and again cried, "Where is he?"

Misam was almost hysterical and was speaking so fast that no one could understand her. Hadiza put her arm around her daughter's shoulders and said, "Now close your eyes and take a deep breath and tell us what happened." Misam did as her mother instructed and was calmer almost instantly. She forced herself to slow down and said, "The priests and some soldiers chased us and grabbed Lo after he stumbled. I don't know what happened after that. I was running as fast as I could like Lo told me to do. I was just so scared! Momma, I was so scared. What will they do to him? Where could they have taken him? Lo tried to warn me, but I was so busy looking for the right fish for supper that I ignored him. He said, 'That priest is staring at us,' and I just ignored him until it was too late. Oh, God, until it was too late! He tried to run but because of his leg he had problems running, and he stumbled and fell right in front of the soldiers! That saved me from being caught so I kept running as fast as I could until I got to the gate here. I have no idea where they took him."

Right then, Marta's father showed up from the warehouse. Seeing the whole household in the front courtyard and Misam crying, he asked, "What is going on here? Why is Misam crying and why are you all in the front courtyard?"

Marta started to repeat what Misam had said but was interrupted by Misam. "Lo has been taken by the priests and their soldiers. He tried to run, and he stumbled, and they caught him."

Akeem asked, "Run? Why? Misam, tell me from the beginning what happened. Don't leave out the smallest detail."

She explained what happened at the fish market and what happened to Lo. He looked at her intently. "Are you sure you or Lo didn't do anything out of the ordinary?"

Misam shook her head and insisted, "No, nothing. Lo is always so careful, especially when those priests are around. I was shopping and looking at different tables of fish and he was watching the crowd like he always does. I didn't even notice the priests until Lo told me about one watching us."

Akeem acted a little irritated and asked, "A priest was watching you? I told you to tell me everything, even the tiniest detail. The details are important. Tell me again everything that happened from the time you left the house till you got back." Misam went over the events again and again, as well as she could remember them. Marta's father grilled her on the tiniest details until he was satisfied that there were no more details to tell. He could see she was getting tired and looked at Hadiza and said, "Take her in the house and get her some food and wine." He looked at Misam. "Thank you, you were very helpful. Those details told me a lot, and I think I know where Lo is being held. I must go to the king to fix this. I hope he can help me. Those priests have a lot of political power, and I am not sure what sway the king has over them, but I will find out right now. He looked at Almed's servant and said, "Come with me."

He and the servant started off toward the palace at a quick walk. They arrived at the palace in about a short while later. A guard stopped them at the gate, and Akeem told the guard that he had urgent business with the king, and if the guard would announce Akeem's arrival, he was sure the king would see him. The guard was hesitant at first, but when Akeem said, "I am the linen merchant, the one that turned in the tax collector." The guard knew instantly that the king would probably see him without delay. The story of the foreign linen merchant that got the better of a crooked tax collector was an often repeated story among the soldiers and guards. They all despised tax collectors, especially dishonest ones, and unfortunately, most were dishonest. The guard ran into the king's court and over to the captain of the army who was standing next to the king and whispered Marta's father requests to see the king. The captain then went over to the king and whispered the information to the king. The king had been listening to a dispute between two of the wealthiest ship owners in Ashkelon for quite a while and was getting rather bored with their back-and-forth bantering. So an excuse to put them on hold, even for a short while, delighted him and knowing it was Akeem made it even better.

He interrupted their arguing and said, "You two, hold up. I have some important business to attend to, and I will need you to go outside until I call you back in a short while." With that, the king signaled the two guards standing next to him to escort the two men out a side door. He looked at the captain and said, "Bring my friend in. Tell him I would be delighted to see him."

Akeem and Almed's servant came in at a quick pace, which surprised the king. Usually, Akeem walked with slow, deliberate steps, and with a confidence that the king admired. The king asked, "What is it, my friend? What emergency brings you here today? By your demeanor, I suspect that there is a dire issue happening."

The father answered in a hurried voice, "My daughter's servant has been taken by a couple priests. I fear they have very bad intentions. Two of our servants, a male and a female, were at the fish market and apparently caught the attention of the priests, and the priests sent some soldiers after them and caught the male servant. This servant is an Egyptian and has been instrumental in the success of the business. He is a small, thin man that poses no threat to anyone. Can you help me get him freed?"

The king stood up. "Do you know for sure it was priests that took him?"

Akeem answered, "Yes, our female servant saw one standing over Lo while two soldiers held him down."

The king replied cautiously, "Priests don't just grab someone unless there has been some sort of insult to Baal, or the person was acting in a dangerous manner."

Akeem insisted. "Lo is a small-framed man, not given to violence. He's more of an intellectual than a fighter. I can't see him creating a disturbance in any way. It would be incredibly unusual. He went on to say, "The girl servant with him said he told her he saw a priest watching them, and it made him uneasy. He instructed her to avert her eyes from looking in the priest's direction. I think he knew something was amiss, but the female servant was insistent on finishing her shopping. No, I sincerely believe he was targeted for some other reason—for what reason, I don't know."

The king looked down for a few minutes and said, "I have had enough of these priests and especially the high priest. He thinks he is the king, and I am just a figure head that he tolerates, well, those days are over."

He called for the captain of his army to come. "Bring the high priest to me. If he resists arrest him, tie him up and drag him if you must. I am tired of him thinking he is a shadow king. Bring him to me at once. If anyone else gets in the way, kill them. Don't arrest them, kill them! They are defying an order of the king, so make an example of them. I want the high priest alive though. Let your soldiers know that if anyone kills the priest, that person will forfeit his life and the lives of his family."

The soldier stated that he understood, bowed, and left running. The king turned to Akeem. "The high priest has been getting more and more carried away with himself. I should have put a stop to it long ago, but the people are protective of their priests, and I wanted to keep the peace as long as they didn't get out of hand. He has now gotten out of hand, and I intend to put a stop to it—today!"

The captain arrived at the high priest's house with one hundred soldiers. He had twenty soldiers at each end of the street to block the street and posted the rest near the front door of the house. The captain had one of the soldiers knock on the door and wait. A servant came to the door, and ten soldiers forced their way into the house with the captain right behind them. The high priest and two other priests along with two soldiers came from the courtyard into the house to confront the intruders. The high priest was surprised when the saw the captain among the intruders. He demanded loudly, "What is the meaning of this intrusion into my home?" The high priest yelled out of hopes of intimidating the soldiers. It didn't work. Two of the soldiers grabbed him and began to tie him up. One of the other priests tried to interfere and one of the captain's soldiers ran him through with his sword. The fatally injured priest shuddered and fell. The other priest and his accompanying soldiers backed up and then left the room.

With that, the high priest stopped resisting. The high priest looked at the captain and demanded, "What is the meaning of this heresy? You know who I am and what I can have done to you for this treasonous act of heresy. Now I insist that you let me go this instant."

The captain slapped him across the face and commanded him, "Silence, or I will personally cut out your tongue and enjoy every minute of it. I have never liked you and I am relishing this moment. Because of you my cousin is dead, and now I get to see justice. Yes, I am definitely relishing this moment."

With that, they started their way back to the palace. A crowd started to gather at each end of the street, and when the high priest saw them, he thought it was an opportunity to be freed, so he yelled out, "Help me, heretics are defiling my house! They have actually killed a priest and are going to kill me, help me!" A dozen people tried to intervene, but the soldiers were brutal, killing several and wounding several more. The crowd disbursed, and the soldiers formed up in two double lines. Fifty in front and fifty behind.

The captain walked up to the priest and said, "If the king had not given me explicit orders, I would have killed you right here. But he has something special planned for you." The captain laughed. "Yes, he has something very special planned I think." The way the captain said it struck panic in the priest. He knew that he was on the edge of death and was trying to figure why and think of a way out of his situation. He knew that the way all this came about told him that he was probably a dead man anyway. That he had crossed some line, and he was not sure what it was.

The priest thought to himself, *Could it possibly have something to do with that revolting Egyptian heretic they arrested this morning? Why would the king be interested in a foreign heretic?*

The captain walked in a hurry, and when the priest slowed down at all, the captain shoved him with brutal force. The priest stumbled and turned to the captain and demanded, "You will treat me with the dignity of a high priest of Baal. I will not tolerate being treated like a criminal." It was more said out of bluff than true authority. He had become accustomed to ordering people about thinking the king wouldn't dare cross a priest of Baal. Again, he was wrong.

They arrived at the palace, and the captain ordered the soldiers to stand fast while he went to the king to announce their arrival. He rushed past the king's guards and into the courtyard where the king was waiting. The king stood up when he saw the captain and asked, "Was there much trouble? Did anybody try to stop you?"

The captain responded, "A few tried, sire, even a priest tried, but he found himself at the sharp end of a sword. The chief priest tried to get some of the crowd to set him free, but they also found themselves at the wrong end of a sword. I believe five or six paid the ultimate price for their insolence, but the incident was quickly quelled. We didn't have any more problems after that. I have the priest being held near the front door of the palace. I can bring him in now if you want sire."

The king smiled and said, "No, let him stand out there and stew for a few minutes. Meanwhile have a cup of wine and rest yourself. I have a very important question to ask him, and his answer will determine whether he lives or dies. Have one of your soldiers go ask him if he knows where the Egyptian is that he took prisoner this morning and come back and tell me his answer."

The captain summoned one of his senior soldiers and instructed him to do as the king commanded. The soldier didn't like the priest as well and was more than happy to question him. He immediately went to where the priest was being held and walked up, slapped him, and then asked, "Where is the Egyptian you took prisoner this morning? Answer quickly, your life is on the line." The priest was instantly angry and was going to yell at the soldier until the soldier made the last statement, "Your life is on the line." Now he was truly terrified.

The priest, with some false bravado, said, "He is being held at the temple by my guards. I had instructed them to interrogate him to find out if he was a spy. Why is the king so upset about an Egyptian servant?"

The soldier ignored the question and ran into the courtyard where his captain was and relayed what the priest had said. Then the captain relayed it to the king. The king ordered, "Captain, take your men and go quickly to the temple and retrieve the Egyptian and bring him here to me. Keep the priest standing out front until you have brought me the Egyptian then bring the priest in to me with the Egyptian."

The captain ordered his men into formation and directed them to make double-time to the temple. They arrived at the temple, and the main door was barred, and when the soldiers knocked, no one would open it from the inside. The soldiers took a bench they found near the front door and used it as a battering ram. The door was splintered in three swings of the bench. The captain's soldiers rushed in and were met by ve temple soldiers who were quickly dispatched. They went into a room off the main meeting room and found Lo tied across a table. The priests had beaten him severely and used a cane on him to try and get him to confess that he was a spy. He wouldn't give in, and it nearly cost him his life. He was too injured and weak to walk so the captain had his men construct a stretcher out of two spears and one of the temple curtains. He also had them tie up a three of priests to take with them back to the palace. They hurried back to the palace carrying Lo and with three priests following in tow. The captain and ten soldiers escorted the high priest and the temple priests, and four soldiers carried Lo into the courtyard.

The king ordered the high priest forward. "Who authorized you to arrest this man? Who in this palace gave you permission? Point him out, and I will deal with him. Who?"

The chief priest stammered and was finally able to get out "No one, sire. I thought he was a spy and a heretic, and I took it upon myself to have him arrested."

The king leaned forward and looked at the high priest in the eye and said, "Who gave you this authority?"

The priest straightened his shoulders and said, "No one, sire, I assumed it was part of my duties as the high priest to deal with such people. I've always done so before today."

The king sat back and said, "That is quite an assumption. I would assume in that case, anyone in the kingdom would have such authority, right? I mean you are only trying to protect the kingdom, right? Who could fault that? The only problem is that if a person hated his neighbor, then he claims he was only trying to protect the kingdom and could do what he willed with the offending neighbor, right? In this case, though, the person arrested was the servant of a friend of mine. A very good friend of mine. The Egyptian looks as if he is in bad condition." He turned to Akeem and said, "My friend, why don't you see that he is tended to by one of the palace doctors while I deal with this priest."

Akeem went immediately to Lo and assessed how badly he was injured. Lo had several deep cuts on his face and back. It appeared that a couple of his fingers were broken. He was weak and in terrible pain. Another hour in the priest's hands, and Akeem was sure Lo would have been dead. He and Almed's servant assisted the doctors in tending Lo's injuries. Akeem asked Lo jokingly, "Why is it that you are the only one who finds the hard end of a long stick? Marta is not going to be happy with you."

Lo responded, "I keep finding people with a bigger stick than mine. I think I'll just stay home for the rest of the time we are here." The two men laughed, and Lo winced. The doctors, who didn't speak Egyptian, could not understand a word but recognized that though badly injured, Lo was going to be all right.

The king had a soldier bring the chief priest up closer to the throne, and then the king leaned forward and whispered, "I really don't like people that assume on my good graces, and I especially don't like you. I knew you were going to be trouble from the first day I met you, and I should have addressed it then, but better late than never." He leaned back and said, "Captain, take this man to the town square, announce his crime, and use a scourge on him to within an inch of his life and then for good measure, execute him. Do it with fanfare, reading the charges against him so all can hear, arresting a man without my authorization, injuring a friend of the king, and resisting the king's soldiers in the performance of their duties. Make sure you have a crowd. I don't want anyone to assume on my graces again. I want this priest to be an object lesson that no matter your station you are my subject and, as such, are subject to my laws."

The high priest called out, "Have mercy, my king, have mercy!"

The king turned to the captain of the army and asked, "Should I have mercy on him? What do you think?"

The captain looked at the high priest and answered, "I think we should show him the same mercy he showed my cousin, sire."

The king said, "I agree, the same level of mercy."

The captain took the high priest, and it was the last time the king ever saw him.

Akeem arranged for four soldiers to carry Lo back to the house and then he stayed to thank the king. The king responded with his hand in the air, "No need to thank me. I have hated that man for a long time. I am just sorry your servant suffered because I didn't deal with him before this. He had one of thecaptain's cousins tortured to death. I figured the cousin must have violated some religious rule, and for the sake of keeping the peace, I did nothing. I was wrong in that instance as well, but now I had an opportunity to make up for that wrong. I don't think you will be having any more problems from the priests. If they do cause you any trouble, let me know and I will handle it."

Akeem bowed. "I thank you, sire, and I am forever in your debt."

And with that, Akeem returned home to find the whole house fussing over Lo.

Misam ran to Marta's father and hugged him. "Thank you for saving him, thank you."

Seeing this, Marta realized there was more to Misam's reaction than simple concern for Lo; may be romantic affection was at the bottom of her reaction as well as concern. Marta walked over and hugged her father as well and said, "I don't know how you did it, but thank you for saving Lo. I am sure they would have killed him. Imagine they thought he was a spy. We have been living here for years now, so who would he be spying for? All this for a stupid assumption. What did the king do to the priest?"

"Let's just say you will never have to worry about that man again."

"I will always worry as long as that man is alive," Marta lamented.

"Exactly," her father replied with a sober look on his face.

17

What's Happening at Home

Marta slowly started to take over the management of the house in Ashkelon but not without some grumbling from Almed's servants. She put a quick stop to that with a bit of wisdom, a moderate amount of bluster, and her well known ability to remind the staff of each person's station in the house. Almed was supportive and explained that she was the wisest and most shrewd person he had ever met and to be on her side was not only wise but imperative to having a smooth-running household—and because he said so.

Days turned into weeks and then months, then into years. Marta and her father sent Gamal and one of Almed's servants back to Shunem several times a year with food and money for Marta's brothers and for Ishaman and the rest of Marta's servants. All appeared in order, though Ishaman told them about the hardships most of the region was suffering, but thanks to the food and money Marta was sending them, he was able to take care of the livestock and the servants that stayed behind to help. He told Gamal that there had been some trouble, but he and the other servants were able drive off the troublemakers, although not without some loss of life and of livestock. He failed to mention the livestock that he sold for exorbitant sums of money, which he kept. After hearing Ishaman's news, Akeem wanted to check on the houses in Shunem himself and took Gamal and Almed's servant with him. The three of them stayed off the road as much as possible due to the presence of bandits around almost every turn. They arrived in Shunem at the worst of the famine. For safety's sake, they stayed out of the town

162

until after dark. Nearly a quarter of the town had died of starvation and disease. The land was dry and barren. Nearly all the trees were dead. It was eerily quiet in town, not even the birds were singing. No roosters crowing. No cows or livestock of any kind were anywhere to be seen except at his daughter's house, and even then, there were very few left.

When he asked Ishaman where the rest of the animals were, he said, "There was a group of armed men from the town that came to the farm and attacked us. We were able to hold the men off by fortifying the largest barn and saved some of the animals, but several were taken, and I suppose were eaten. Also,they killed one of the mistress's servants, now there are six of us left. This famine has gone on for five years now. The people are starving. It is truly a terrible situation. I wish we had been able to go with all of you."

They went to Akeem's house to check on Marta's brothers and their families. It was there that they received some heartbreaking news about lifetime friends that had died. The midwife, mother's best friend since childhood, died from some ailment brought on by starvation. Several of their friends left for other cities. Some never made it to another town, dying either starvation or bandits. Marta's brothers were doing fine, thanks to the food and money Gamal brought on a quarterly basis. Nobody bothered them like they did Ishaman.

Akeem and the two servants returned to Ashkelon shaken. Marta and his wife met him, anxiously waiting for news from home; he looked at them with deeply sad eyes, "Many of our friends are dead, and the ones that are not, are not the same as when we left them. I tried to tell them. I told them what the prophet said, and they ignored me. I wish I could have done more."

Marta's mother cried off and on for over an hour after finding out her best friend from childhood was dead as well as most of her friend's family. She lamented, "My friend, my wonderful friend gone," she cried over and over. The group started to feel some guilt about how well they had faired through the crisis compared to their hometown.

Finally, Marta spoke up and said, "They were warned and decided to stay, and even when the famine hit, they still decided to stay. When people are that stubborn, there is nothing anyone can do. Even if we wanted to help, we couldn't do enough to make a difference. There are just too many people, and the situation just too terrible. When we get back, we will do what we can, but that is nearly two years away. We will send more food for our family and the servants that are still there, but that is the extent of what we can do. When we send the servants with food, it must be with the utmost stealth. People are desperate, and even the best of friends cannot be trusted. It is truly a life-and-death environment."

Her father replied, "She's right. Let's just do what we can to live here peaceably, and when we get back, we will do what we can for our friends then. Right now, we are very limited in what we can do to help without causing a riot or, worse yet, losing everything we have left there. All we can do is do the best we can to survive here."

At his palace, the king of Ashkelon was beside himself on how well things were working out in the linen business and how his tax revenue was up by 30 percent now that he had an honest tax collector. The prior tax collector, turned servant for Almed, was reported to be a shell of himself. The guard from Almed's house would give a report to the king weekly and a report on Almed as well. Though he liked and trusted Akeem, he still was not able to fully trust Almed.

The once-tax collector was not causing any trouble and seemed to have settled into the household routine, but his seething rage was starting to get the better of him, and he was secretly becoming more dangerous each day. He never talked to the other servants and glared at them until corrected by the king's guard. The guard sensed there was a growing animosity between the other servants and the tax collector and began to watch him more closely.

Lo was teaching Eli and Marta every day. His wounds and fingers had healed, but his leg never returned to normal. He walked with a more pronounced limp, and occasionally, the leg would swell and cause him excruciating pain. Marta worried about him and decided that he was exempt from hard physical labor. He could teach but no more trips to the market, and he was not to carry heavy things or even help clean the house. None of the other servants resented that decision, except for the tax collector.

Despite some small issues, things were going quite well until one day the once-tax collector got into a run-in with Hadiza. She told him to help bring some food in from a cart in the courtyard, and he exploded. "No woman is going to ever order me around again! I am a man, and no woman is going to treat me like a slave, I won't have it."

Almed stepped in the argument and told him, "You will do whatever she tells you, do you understand?"

The tax collector lost all restraint and attacked Almed, but he found out that Almed was tremendously strong and stopped him with one blow. The king's guard grabbed the tax collector and dragged him into the courtyard and asked Almed what he wanted to do with him. Almed was furious and almost asked the guard to pull his sword and do away with him right then but decided against it.

The guard, seeing the level of anger that Almed was in, said, "Bear in mind that the king spared this man's life once before and ordered that if he caused any problems that he was to die. What do you want me to do? I could take him out in the street and dispatch him right now. What would you like me to do with him?" Almed looked at the tax collector and saw that he was completely unrepentant and said, "This man can never be trusted while alive."

He stopped talking for a second and, rubbing his chin, started to smile, "I have an idea, though, if you will relay it to the king. Let this once-tax collector be made a galley slave on one of the king's ships, with special orders that he always be chained." The guard smiled and said, "He might live a year, but in his current health, I doubt it. I think the king will like your request, at least then he will be worth something while he is alive. However long that may be. Especially under the driver's whip."

The look of defiance on the tax collector's face turned into panic. "I'm sorry. I just lost my temper. It will never happen again. I promise, I will never get out of line again!" Ignoring the man's pleas, the guard dragged him off to his fate.

But before he left, the guard turned to Almed and said soberly, "My only regret is that I will no longer be staying here. You all have treated me like family, and I will always remember you with great affection. Goodbye."

Almed responded, "You have also become like family, you are welcome in my house anytime."

Marta was relieved that the tax collector was gone and was thankful that no one was hurt in the process. She sighed and said, "I, for one, am glad he is out of the house—he was a terrible man." All the servants breathed a sigh of relief as well. They could taste the tension in the air for months and that was gone now.

The remaining two years passed without incident. Marta's father was richer than he had ever been. The household was healthy and thriving. Lo's leg was slowly improving. Eli was now eighteen years old and nearly a man. He was tall like his mother, and he had his mother's gray eyes and black hair. He was broad-chested and muscular like his grandfather Akeem. He had almost none of the physical characteristics of his father. His grandfather had taken him under his wing and was teaching him the linen business.

One day, Akeem came to Marta and Eli and said, "I need you both to come with me. It is extremely important. Don't ask questions please, just trust me." They followed her father through winding streets to the city gates, and sitting there were several elders Marta had come to know over the years and some that she had never met before. Also sitting there on a rather elaborate chair turned throne was the king of Ashkelon. Eli looked at his mother with a look of fear and confusion. Marta herself was getting nervous. She turned to Akeem and asked, "What is going on, Father? I'm not sure I like this."

Akeem turned and smiled, "Trust me."

The three of them stopped, and all except the king stood up to greet them. Akeem said with a loud voice, "Sire, elders, and servants of the king, I am delighted to introduce my grandson Eli, in whom I am well pleased. He can now do business in my name. Eli has proven himself to be a hard and honest worker. I trust him in all my business, and I ask you to trust him as you would me. Whatever he binds in my name is bound and whatever he promises in my name is my promise. I am so immensely proud of him on this day. I brought to you Eli the boy, and now I declare him Eli the man." The men came around the shocked boy now turned man and patted him on the back and ceremoniously introduced themselves. They all stopped when the king stood up and approached Eli.

The king exclaimed, "You will forever from this day be invited into my court and to my table as a friend of the king. Your grandfather has over the years proven himself as a benefit to me and a man of the highest integrity. He is a friend of the king and now you are as well."

The king looked at Marta and said to Akeem, "Is this the woman I have heard so much about. The words that they used to describe her beauty were understated. If it were not for our traditions that forbid me to marry a foreigner, I would have you as my wife. I hear your wisdom is unmatched in any kingdom. It is an honor to meet you at last."

Marta was stunned but held her composure and bowed. "Sire, I am so honored that you even know of my existence. I am just a humble widow and mother. I am so very grateful for your words and for how you have received our family. The thought that the king himself would come and honor my son in such a manner is beyond words. You are truly as great a man as my father describes."

The king smiled and bowed to Marta who bowed back but lower.

There were some festivities that the king had put together, and afterward while returning home, Marta slapped her father on his shoulder. "You rascal, you! You caught Eli and I both completely by surprise. The king! The king himself came to honor Eli! This is the most wonderful day of my life except when Eli was born."

Eli walked quietly beside his grandfather when his mother asked, "Well, do you have anything to say? Sis is literally the most important day of your life. You have just been declared a man."

Eli stopped, turned, and hugged his grandfather. "I will never in my lifetime have the words to describe how I feel right now. If I live to be a hundred, I will tell of this day to my children and their children. I plan to one day perform this bit of surprise on them. Imagine, today I am officially a man. Mother, I am a man today!"

Marta looked at him with pride and said, "Today, you may officially be a man but always remember that I am still and always will be officially your mother." She hugged him and under her breath said, "Thank you, Prophet. Thank you, God, of the prophet. Thank you."

They returned to the house and found that Almed had prepared a feast. To keep the event a surprise for both Eli and Marta, he had the food prepared at friends' houses and had his and Marta's servants help. They had all kept it a secret until that day. The feast lasted well into the night. Even the king's guard had come to help them celebrate.

The next day, Akeem made an announcement that he was sending Gamal and Lamel to Shunem to see how things were progressing there as it was now time to make plans to return home. Three days later, the men set out for Shunem. They arrived without a problem and intended to stay out of the town until dark but from a distance could see the town was now bustling. There were carts on the road with fresh produce on them, and some carts were literally over owing with hay and different foods. There were still signs of the havoc wreaked by the famine, but they could see that things were returning to normal. They came into the town and found the streets were full of life, though some of the houses stood empty. The famine had taken its toll, but life was coming back to Shunem.

They came to Akeem's house and found it well kept, and all inside were well. His sons and grandchildren ran out and hugged them and pulled him into the house. He asked the sons how they were doing, and they said it was tense at times. Toward the end of the famine, people figured out they had food and tried to storm the front gate, but they drove them off. Unfortunately, they had to kill three of the invaders that used to be neighbors, some of whom had at one time been family friends.

"It was a sad day, yes, a very sad day," the oldest son lamented. He went on to say, "There are strange happenings at Marta's house. When we went there to check and see if everyone was all right, we were chased off by one of the king's soldiers with no explanation. He just told us to leave, so we did. We figured it would all be straightened out when you returned."

The men went to Marta's house and to their relief found it intact and everything in its place, but something was off. Looking for Ishaman, they went to the largest barn where Ishaman's room was and found it empty. They went to the house, knocked on the door, and Ishaman came to the door and commanded a couple of servants to throw the two off the land. When Gamal protested, they were met by one of the king of Shunem's soldiers, and he told them to leave. Gamal was confused and a bit dazed by this turn of events. They went back to Akeem's house and asked his son's if they knew about

Ishaman taking over the house. Some friends had told them that Ishaman had documents that stated that Marta had turned the farm over to him and went to the king's representatives and some of the elders of Shunem to make it official. Since no one had seen Marta in years, the elders as well as the king assumed that Ishaman was telling the truth. Cutting their visit short, Gamal was now in a hurry to get back and relay this information to Marta and her father.

They pressed hard, and five days later, when they returned to Ashkelon, they found that Akeem was gone for a couple of weeks to Tyre to sell some linen cloth. He was not expected back for another two days. When Marta heard the news about her house, she was incensed. She immediately made plans to return to Shunem and set her affairs in order. She explained things to Almed and then left the next morning with Eli, Gamal, and Lamel. She even outpaced Eli. She was tired, but she was angrier than she was tired and didn't slack her pace the entire trip. They stayed with her brothers the day they arrived; and the next morning they, brothers and all, went to the farm. Ishaman was waiting for them. He had heard they were in town and was ready for them. Marta walked up to him and demanded, "Explain yourself. What are you doing in my house and who gave you permission to move into my house? You knew I was going to return."

Ishaman crossed his arms and stated, "This is no longer your house. I have documents showing that you gave the house and property to me, duly witnessed by two of the city elders. Soldier, I told you she would be coming to cause trouble, and here she is. Do as the king has commanded."

The soldier stepped between Marta and Ishaman and said, "The king commanded that if you were to return and cause problems, he would have you thrown in prison. Now either you leave, or I will escort you and your servants to the prison." He lied. Marta looked the soldier straight in the eye and was going to say something but decided if it was the kings command, that the soldier was only doing as he was commanded, and in that, she would lose the battle if she protested too much right now. Her only hope was to go to the king herself. She wheeled around and signaled Gamal and the others to come with her. Eli, Gamal, Lamel, and her brothers were ready to fight, but Marta knew that would be futile.

She snapped at them, "Follow me now! We are leaving! Now!" The five men were fuming.

Eli said, "I want to go back and beat Ishaman to within an inch of his life."

Marta shrugged. "He thinks he got away with it but there is a king that I need to talk to."

Eli said, "No, I will go and talk to the king and demand our land back."

Marta laughed. "Demand! You will just walk up to the king and stomp your foot and say, 'Give me back my land'? He would have you executed in a minute. No, you will go with me as an escort, but you will keep silent. Do you understand?"

Eli bit his lower lip and eventually said, "I understand. I don't like it, but I understand."

Then Marta smiled and continued, "I did not suffer all that I have suffered only to have a thief steal it from me and, more importantly, from my son. I am more afraid of failing my son than I am of dying. I will fight Ishaman to the death if I must, but he is not taking my son's inheritance without a fight. A fight to the death if it has to be that way, but I am not giving up."

Gamal spoke up. "Wouldn't it be better to wait until your father could help?"

Marta replied, "It would be at least a month before he could get here, and by the time my father could get here, Ishaman will have fortified his political position with the entire city. No, I need to act now!"

18
Restored

The king of Shunem had heard of this Jewish prophet for years but has never met him. He heard that the prophet was in the city and sent messengers to invite him to the palace. The region was doing better after the famine but was still in some distress, and he wanted to see if there was any way the prophet Elisha could help. Perhaps he could intercede and plead with his God to somehow help them overcome the famine quicker. He heard that Gehazi, the wine merchant's son, served the prophet, and perhaps Gehazi could help convince the prophet to intercede.

When the king's messengers went to Mt. Carmel, met Elisha and invited him to the palace, Elisha accepted the invitation without hesitation. Gehazi was surprised that his master accepted. "Sir, you never come when anyone summons you. Not even when the king of Judah called on you to come did you accept. Why now?"

Elisha smiled. "There is a purpose for me to be there, and it has only partly to do with their king. You will see. Have faith, you will see."

When they got to the king's palace, the king was sitting in a large chair on the front porch of the palace. There were ten stairs that ascended to the porch. The porch was twenty feet wide and thirty feet long with a large column on each side. There were about one hundred people waiting near the porch. Many were either servants of the king or elders invited by the king to see and hear Elisha speak. But there were many people there that had come for various

171

other reasons. Some were there to settle disputes; some were there with guards around them and chains on them for various criminal infractions. But there was this one very notable person that seemed out of place. A lady and her son standing in the crowd that Gehazi missed but the prophet did not. His eyes locked on hers, and he smiled. She smiled back with tears welling up in her eyes.

When Elisha and Gehazi arrived in the king's court, the king motioned them to come up next to him and started to ask Elisha questions. Gehazi interrupted and said, "I beg your pardon, sire, but he does not speak our language, but I can interpret for you both if you wish."

The king was a little perturbed at being interrupted and said, "Yes, yes, I wish it. I wish it. Interpret for the both of us, thank you."

Gehazi told Elisha what was said, and Gehazi explained and asked if he could give a brief history of Elisha's accomplishments. With a smile, Elisha asked, "What will you tell him? That I am an old man with a walking stick, and I travel a lot?"

Gehazi smiled back and said, "That, and a few more things if you don't mind." The prophet smiled at the "If you don't mind," remembering when they first met on the road to Shunem so long ago, and said, "Not at all, tell him what you feel is best." And as Gehazi was telling the king of many of the exploits and miracles he had seen at the hands of the prophet, he came to the part where Elisha raised a Shunammite woman's son from the dead. Gehazi was speaking loud enough so the whole crowd could hear. As he was talking, he scanned the crowd to see their reaction, and as he did, he saw the lady and her son. He stopped and stood erect and pointed them out to the king. He exclaimed in a loud voice, "Sire, there is the lady and her son who Elisha raised from the dead."

The king looked and noticed her right away. He stood up and stepped toward her and stared with amazement. He said in a low tone, "Marta, is that you?" Then with a louder voice, "Marta is that really you? Is what Gehazi saying about your son being raised from the dead true? Did this really happen?"

Her tears were owing freely now, "Yes, sire, it is true. The prophet raised my son from death into life, and this is the son. His name is Elisha. My father Akeem and I named him after the prophet.

I will always be in the prophet's debt. He did what no one else could do. He raised my son from the dead and brought my dreams back from the dead as well."

The king smiled with tears in his eyes said, "Please call me by the name I gave you long ago."

She smiled and said, "Jal, I have missed my friend so much. I'm sorry I wasn't there to see you crowned king, forgive me."

While she was talking, the king kept his gaze fixed on her in amazement. Then he turned to Elisha, and the king started to understand that this is not just a man who was famous for doing "tricks" but is a man that command the very angles of heaven. A tinge of fear ran down his back. He was thinking that maybe inviting this man to the palace was not such a good idea. He didn't like not feeling completely in charge. He was the king, and this man didn't even have nice clothes to wear to an audience with the king. Yet he knew that crossing this man would be extremely dangerous even for a king. Needless to say, there was a presence about the man that was somewhat intimidating.

The king cleared his mind and his throat and went on to say, "I remember that you were married to that despicable man, Saana. I always disliked the man. He was a good businessman but a terrible person at the same time. No one misses him. Pardon me, but I had no heartbreak when I heard he died. You are very exceptional indeed for having survived a marriage to a man such as he." Then tenderly looking at her, he said, "From the first day we met by the stream, I knew that something very special was happening." Then noticing that Elisha and Gehazi were watching intently and that they admired this woman immensely, he turned back to her and said, "I am so happy to see you. You can't know how happy, but I have to ask, why are you here? What matter brought you here?"

Marta was still very emotional and had to collect her thoughts. Then he tenderly asked, "Well, go on, my Marta, tell me why you are here."

She was finally able to put the words together, "Seven years ago, I was warned about the famine by the prophet here, and I have been in Ashkelon until now. I came home to Shunem to check on the affairs of my house and found my head field servant had deceived some of the elders in the community and some of the king's representatives into falsifying documents that stated I had given him my house and all my property." With the words "some of the king's representatives," a few of them in the crowd started to squirm. They had no idea that Marta was a close friend of the king and now were in shock. They had accepted bribes to falsify the documents because they never expected the owner to return.

The king looked toward them and asked, "Is this true? Did some of you help this man steal this woman's property?"

One of the representatives came forward and said, "The man's arguments appeared to be legitimate. Had we known they were not we would never have agreed to help him. She had been gone for several years, and there was no reason to doubt his authenticity."

The king leaned forward and said, "So you agreed with the man who stole this woman's property." The man was now shaking with fear, "Yes, sire. But as I was saying, only because we were deceived, but we would have never helped him. He came to us with false assertions, and since she had been gone so long, there was no other way to verify them, so we believed him."

The king looked over to the captain of the army and said, "I want you to investigate this, but before you do that, take this woman back to her house and arrest the thief. Also, any profit he may have made since she has been gone is to be returned to her." He then turned to the Marta and asked, "You were gone how long?"

She answered, "Seven years, sire."

The king sat back down and commanded, "Have him return all seven years proceeds from the land to her, going back to the day she left."

The captain bowed. "Consider it done, sire," and then turned to Marta and motioned that she follow him.

When they arrived back to Marta's house, Ishaman was standing on the front porch with the soldier next to him. When the soldier saw the captain walking in front of Marta, he stepped back. Ishaman was confused by his reaction. Ishaman ordered the soldier like he was a servant, "What is the problem? Throw this lady and her friends off my property!"

The soldier walked up to his captain and said, "I am here because this lady claims this property is hers, but this man has documents proving the property is his. I was only here by request of one of the king's representatives to enforce the law."

The captain asked in a low voice that only the soldier could hear. "Didn't you tell this lady that the king himself gave you orders to throw her off this property?" The soldier stood there red-faced and unable to answer. the captain said with a stern voice, "Step aside, soldier. I will deal with you later."

Ishaman realized that he was in serious trouble when he saw the soldier was deeply afraid of this man. In trying to control the situation, he demanded, "Who are you to order this soldier of the king?" The captain walked to within an arm's length from Ishaman and said, "I am the captain of the king's army, and who are you, or better yet who do you think you are? I am here to set things in order. I am here to take this woman's property back for her. Not only that, but take back the last seven years proceeds, starting from the day she left."

Ishaman raised his voice, "Take back seven years' proceeds! Take back the property! We will just see what the king has to say about all this."

The captain shouted out, "Idiot, the king is who sent me. And now, it is my pleasure to say, you are under arrest." The captain turned to the soldier who had kicked Marta off her own property and commanded, "Soldier, bind this man and take him back to the palace with us."

He turned to Marta and said, "My lady, the house is yours and anything you find in it. This man will be in prison until he pays all that is due to you. The king's representatives have a lot to answer for, but be assured you will have no problems from them again. I know the king is going to ask a lot of questions such as where the document came from. I doubt that this man can read or write so someone had to write the document for him. Now that brings up another question: Did he pay a bribe to the king's representatives? I will find this out in good time, but for now, your property is yours again. If I can be of any more service, just let me know, and I will send one of my soldiers at once. I can see that you have truly found favor with the king."

Ishaman started to say something, and the soldier slapped him and told him to keep silent. He was trying to appear as a true soldier of the king and maybe redeem himself somewhat. That was the last time Marta ever saw Ishaman, the chief field servant, again.

When the four of them went into the house, they saw that Ishaman had kept it neat and clean and had actually done several improvements. She turned to the men and said, "We are home. It's time to move back and pick up our lives where we left off. We will rest a day and return to Ashkelon to pack and come back to our house."

The next morning, Eli was walking around the barns, inspecting the livestock and talking with the field servants when he saw Elisha and Gehazi walking on the road toward the house. He immediately ran to the house and announced, "Elisha is coming!" All four of them came out of the house to greet the prophet.

"Good morning," Marta said with a singsong voice. "It is good to see you. Thank you, Gehazi, for what you did for us yesterday."

Gehazi responded, "All I did was to tell the king the story of your son being raised from the dead. I didn't know about your problems until you told the king. I am so very happy that it all worked out." Then he laughed and said, "I forgot that you knew the king when he was prince, amazing."

Elisha said through Gehazi, "We will be coming through this way occasionally to check on how you are doing, but I suspect you will do very well from now on. If not, you know where to find me." He finished with a sly grin.

She replied, "Yes, indeed I know where to find you, and I hope to bring Eli there some day."

Elisha responded, "You can come and visit any time. You are always welcome in my house." Elisha then turned into his room and Gehazi went to visit his father.

Marta sat down and put her arm around Eli and said, "This is a good life. There are many trials, for sure, but truly life is good." Then she looked up into the sky and said, "It's a very good life after all." Eli looked at his mother and smiled and hugged her. To her, that hug was the best thing she had ever felt in her life. They then turned and went back into the house.

The next day, there was a loud knock at the front door. Gamal answered it, and there was the captain of the army with a couple of his soldiers. Gamal bowed and said, "Come in, come in. How may I help you?"

The captain smiled and said, "Your mistress is quite a woman. She impressed everyone in the palace, and more importantly, she is a friend of the king. He explained to me the role she played in his life when he was sixteen. He adores her. So much so that he would like to invite her to eat at his table with him today. May I speak to the lady of the house?"

Gamal bowed and said, "Please come in, and I will let her know you are here." Gamal went to Marta and told her what the captain said. She went to him immediately and pressed him about how the king was faring. She smiled and said, "What does he want from me? Whatever it is, I am at his service, but I only brought the clothes that I have on, and I am not dressed for dinner with the king."

The captain laughed and said, "My noble lady, he was so happy to see you again and especially with your son. He wants to talk and have you share your adventures since you last saw each other. He couldn't care less about what you wear. He just wants to see his dear friend. Also, he would like to hear more about your association with the prophet."

The captain looked down and said, "Actually, mistress, his wife died of a plague two years ago during the famine, and I truly believe he has very high regard for you and would desire you to become his queen. Please say nothing to him about this. He is my friend as well as my king. I have known him for many years and have not seen him so captivated by a lady as he is by you. After you left, he acted as if he were a young man again. Full of joy, he patted everyone on the back and kept saying, 'That's my friend, my very best friend.' Please do him and me the favor by accepting his invitation. More than anything, he would take great delight in seeing his friend of so many years."

She reflected for a moment, her beautiful gray eyes gazing upward, remembering the question the prophet asked so long ago, "Would you like me to speak to the king or the commander of the army on your behalf?"

She thought to herself, *You knew, didn't you, Prophet? You knew all along.* She looked the captain square in the eyes, smiled, and decisively answered, "Tell my friend Jal, king of Shunem, I humbly accept his invitation."

ABOUT THE AUTHOR

Don Anderson and his wife Pam of fifty-three years live in Redmond, Oregon, and have two sons and five grandchildren.

Soon after retiring from the US Air Force, where Don spent twenty years on active duty, ten years as a medic, four years as a medical professionals recruiter, and his last six years as a first sergeant for fighter squadrons, he became a chaplain for a psychiatric hospital in Panama City, Florida, and not long after that became an associate pastor in a church in Panama City, Florida, and then was a senior pastor in Springfield, Oregon. He is currently very active in his local church.

While in the Air Force, he was stationed in Saudi Arabia during Desert Storm during the wind down of the war and was able to get to know many of the locals. In getting to know the people, through them, he learned what many of the social customs for both contemporary times and in ancient Middle Eastern history, which helped him immensely in understanding how people there see life so differently then and now.

9 781969 422188